ADVENTURE ISLAND

THE MYSTERY
OF THE KING'S RANSOM

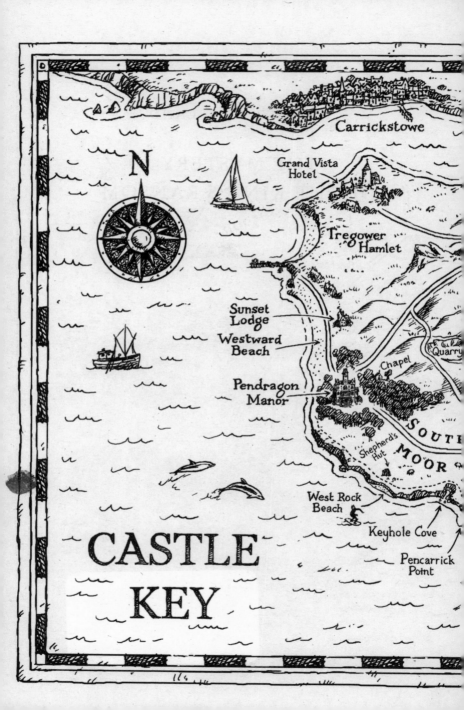

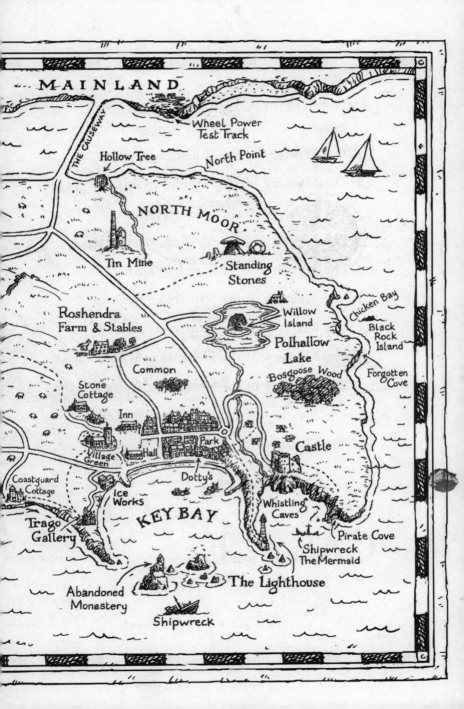

Collect all the Adventure Island *books*

ADVENTURE ISLAND

THE MYSTERY OF THE KING'S RANSOM

Helen Moss

Illustrated by Leo Hartas

Orion
Children's Books

First published in Great Britain in 2013
by Orion Children's Books
a division of the Orion Publishing Group Ltd
Orion House
5 Upper St Martin's Lane
London WC2H 9EA
An Hachette UK company

The Orion Publishing Group's policy is to use papers
that are natural, renewable and recyclable products and made
from wood grown in sustainable forests. The logging and
manufacturing processes are expected to conform to
the environmental regulations of the country of origin.

A catalogue record for this book is
available from the British Library.

Printed in Great Britain by
Clays Ltd, St Ives plc

For Mac, as always

One

A Surprise at Bosgoose Wood

Emily Wild felt a shiver run down her spine. All the way through the woods, birds had been bustling in the trees, squirrels scurrying from branch to branch, bees buzzing in the foxgloves – but here in the clearing there was an eerie silence.

She jumped at a noise in the undergrowth, her heart thumping against her ribs. But it was only Drift – her Right Hand Dog – investigating a rabbit hole. Emily usually avoided Bosgoose Wood, but it was one of the few places on the island that they'd not visited since Scott and Jack had started spending their holidays in Castle Key, and the boys had been keen to explore. They were sauntering along the path behind her now, totally unaware of the creepy atmosphere; they were too busy arguing about who had the most annoying ears, for one thing.

'Here it is!' she announced. 'Bosgoose Cottage.'

Jack sprinted across the glade and ducked through a gap in the old stone wall. The roof had caved in. Emerald-green moss cloaked the jumble of decaying timbers, and spires of pink and yellow weeds sprouted up through the crumbling stone. 'So, what's the story on this place, Em?' he shouted.

'Story?' Emily asked, peering in through a hole that had once been a window. 'What do you mean?'

Jack laughed. 'A deserted cottage in the middle of the deep, dark woods? If I know anything about Castle Key, there has to be *some* sort of ultra-spooky legend about it.'

Emily sank down on the grass and leaned back against a pile of sun-baked stones. 'Not really. The place has been empty for at least fifty years . . .'

'*Not really?*' Jack kicked a heap of dead leaves into the air. 'That means there *is* something!'

'People say the old woman who used to live here was a bit crazy . . .'

'And?' Scott prompted, grinning as he flopped down next to Emily.

Emily sighed. She knew the boys weren't going to let the subject drop. But she also remembered how they'd teased her when they'd thought she was afraid of the midnight ghost last summer, so she did her best to sound casual. 'She was supposed to steal children. It's just one of those silly stories!'

'I *knew* it!' Jack shouted. He'd now scaled the highest remaining section of the cottage wall and was balancing on the top. 'Beware the Crazy Lady of Bosgoose Wood!' he cackled.

'She sounds like the witch in that fairy tale,' Scott said. 'The one who threw kids in her cooking pot. *Goldilocks and the Three Little Pigs,* or something?'

'It was bears, not pigs!' Emily laughed. 'Anyway, you mean *Hansel and Gretel!*'

Up on the wall Jack punched the air. 'Oh, yeah! That means this house should be made of gingerbread.' He took a piece of loose stone from the chimney stack and pretended to bite into it. Then he pretended to spit it out. 'Oh, well, it was worth a try! Which reminds me, there's some of Aunt Kate's banana cake in my backpack.' Jack scrambled back down the wall and handed out slices of cake. 'This place would make an awesome HQ for our next investigation!' he mumbled through a mouthful of crumbs.

Emily smiled. In the bright sunshine, and with the

boys around, Bosgoose Cottage didn't seem creepy at all. A family of rabbits had scampered into the clearing to munch on dandelions, and a pair of swifts was building a nest in a crevice in the cottage wall. And it *would* make a great secret base – there was no danger of anyone overhearing them planning an investigation here. 'That's if we had an investigation to plan!' she sighed.

Scott lay back on the warm grass and chewed on a clover stem. 'Well, I'm in no hurry. In fact, if we *do* come across any mysteries, can't we just report them to the police this time? I've had enough excitement already this summer!'

Emily stared down at him in horror. 'No way!'

'My big brother,' Jack scoffed, 'the world's biggest wimp!'

Scott sat up, grinned, and raked his floppy fringe out of his eyes. 'Only joking! Count me in. Just as long as the next case doesn't involve getting stranded on a collapsing pier in a storm, or dangling from a helicopter with a boatload of Russian gangsters pointing machine guns at me!'

Emily laughed. She had to admit their last case, Operation Skylark, *had* ended in a rather dramatic fashion. 'Don't worry! There's not much chance of any more helicopters or guns this summer.' She pulled her notebook out of her bag, flicked through the empty pages and groaned. 'The way things are going, we'll be lucky to encounter anything riskier than overdue library books and litter louts on the common. It's so annoying! If people are going to commit crimes, why can't they at least make them *interesting* ones . . .'

Emily's words tailed off as she heard the roar of an engine revving. Then there was another, followed by car doors slamming, laughter and shouting voices and a snatch of music.

'What's that?' Jack spun round, dropping his third slice of cake. 'Anyone expecting a surprise party?'

Emily tucked her long brown curls behind her ears to listen. The noise was coming from the north-east. That was strange. There was nothing beyond the woods apart from empty heathland. Beckoning for Jack, Scott and Drift to follow, she darted off along the path through the trees, in the direction of the commotion. She spotted a giant beech tree near the edge of the woods and swung up into the branches. Jack and Scott climbed up behind her. Drift melted into the undergrowth to keep watch.

Peering out through the leaves, the friends had a perfect view of the heath, a mosaic of purple heather, golden gorse and copper-brown bracken, stretching away to the cliffs and the sea beyond, smudging into a hazy blue horizon. Not that Jack noticed the holiday-advert scenery. He was far more interested in the scene closer to hand. Five shiny black jeeps, each bearing a coat of arms and the words BRAITHWAITE BOYS' SCHOOL in gold letters on the side, had been parked in an orderly row. Groups of boys – who looked to be about sixteen – were unloading equipment while their teachers shouted instructions.

'A school camping trip,' Emily whispered.

Only this wasn't like any school camping trip Jack had ever been on – with a beat-up old minibus, a couple of geography teachers and a week's supply of baked beans. It was more like a military operation – or one of those Victorian expeditions with troops of porters lugging soup tureens and four-poster beds through the jungles of Africa. The friends watched in awe as the kit kept appearing – tents the size of mansions, barbecues, inflatable mattresses, pots and pans of every kind, even cake tins and fruit bowls. One of the teachers began setting up a portable generator to run the electrical equipment – enough to stock a medium-sized branch of John Lewis: fridges, lights, fans, televisions.

What next? Jack wondered. *A jacuzzi? A grand piano?*

'That's not proper camping,' Emily giggled. 'You might as well just take your whole house with you!'

'They've no idea how to put that tent up!' Scott commented from his slightly uncomfortable position, wedged into a fork in the tree trunk. He pointed to three boys who were standing with their hands in the pockets of their expensively faded jeans, contemplating a tangle of sagging canvas and twisted tent poles – as if expecting it to magically transform into a fully furnished home-from-home. One of them – a plump, broad-shouldered boy with dark brown skin – tugged on a guy-rope. The ramshackle structure folded to the ground with a *wumpf*. He laughed. Then he looked over his shoulder and whispered something to the other two. One of them grabbed a football from a rack of sports equipment and they all began to slope away from the camp towards the woods.

Scott watched enviously as the boys kicked the football around only metres from the beech tree. He loved football! Two of the boys weren't anything special, but the third – tall and gangly with shaggy brown hair – was obviously a natural, dancing around the others on lightning-fast feet. Scott was on the point of jumping down and asking to join the kickabout when he heard Jack mutter under his breath.

'Uh-oh! Incoming teacher alert!'

A bald man with a sergeant-major-style moustache was striding towards the trio of footballers. He puffed out his chest like a giant pigeon and began yelling at them to get back to work. It was at that moment that Jack's branch began to give way beneath his weight. He grabbed hold of the tree trunk just in time.

Hearing the movement, the sergeant major glanced up – to see the three friends perched among the foliage like a troop of inquisitive monkeys. 'Oi! You lot! Don't let me catch you hanging around here again!' he bellowed.

Emily was speechless with rage. Castle Key was *her* island. She could hang around anywhere she wanted.

But she soon forgot her anger as they headed back through the woods.

Seeing that campsite had given her an amazing idea!

Two

Survival Masterplan

Emily waited until they'd reached the stile on the other side of the woods where they'd left their bikes, before revealing her masterplan to the boys.

'We'll go on a camping trip of our own!' she announced.

Scott considered the idea as they cycled towards Castle Key village. Having left the shade of the trees, it was blisteringly hot, although the narrow track was still muddy after last week's storm. 'Yeah, camping could be fun. Anything's better than listening to you grumble about not having an investigation to work on!' he teased.

Jack stood up on the pedals of his BMX bike to negotiate a deep rut in the track. 'OK, so who's bringing the telly and the fridge?'

Emily laughed. 'No, I mean *proper* camping. Not the luxury version like that Braithwaite School lot.'

Scott grinned. 'There's that ancient canvas tent in Aunt Kate's shed. That's *definitely* not luxury.'

But Emily shook her head. 'No tents!'

'Er, camping without tents?' Jack asked. 'How does that work?'

Scott braked and leaned on his handlebars. He waited for Emily and Jack to pull up next to him. 'You've not been reading the *Survival Guide for Secret Agents* again have you, Em?'

Emily spun her pedal with her toe. 'So what if I have?'

Scott grinned. 'Is there a section in there on surviving in the wilderness, how to collect rainwater, build shelters and all that stuff, by any chance?'

'Exactly! We lash sticks together and cover them with moss and bracken. And we can make beds out of heather and . . .' Emily was so fired up with enthusiasm that she didn't notice Scott and Jack roll their eyes at each other. 'We won't take our phones or any other gadgets. We'll be completely self-reliant.'

18

'Don't tell me,' Jack groaned, 'we live on nothing but grubs and roots and raw fish that we've speared with homemade harpoons?'

'Don't be silly!' Emily laughed.

Jack joined her laughter. 'Phew, that's a relief, for a moment I thought—'

'We'll *cook* the fish over the fire, of course,' Emily said.

'Of course,' Jack echoed, wondering whether he could develop the symptoms of bubonic plague in time to get out of this trip. He didn't even *like* fish!

'And obviously we'll take *some* food with us,' Emily added.

That's more like it! Jack thought. He began planning the menu. He'd make sure they had plenty of bacon, sausages and eggs for fried breakfasts, of course, and he was sure Aunt Kate would supply a selection of flapjacks and muffins. It was well known you had to keep your calorie intake up when involved in outdoor pursuits.

'Just a few basic dried rations for emergencies,' Emily explained.

'So, where shall we go?' Scott asked, swiftly changing the subject before Jack had a meltdown. 'What about Westward Beach?'

Emily shook her head. 'Too crowded. It's got to be somewhere totally isolated where we have to rely on our bushcraft skills to survive.'

Suddenly Scott had an idea. 'What about that island in Key Bay where we found the buried gold?'

'Gulliver's Island!' Emily exclaimed, so excited she nearly dropped her bike. 'Of course! It's perfect. Nobody ever goes there. We'll row there in *Gemini*.'

'Let's go tomorrow!' Scott suggested.

Emily grinned. 'We'll stay for the whole week!'

Scott nodded. 'I'll bring my guitar and we can sing campfire songs!'

'No way!' Emily and Jack shouted in unison.

Drift – who was sitting in his special basket on the back of Emily's bike – joined in with a chorus of barking. He didn't recognize this new word that Emily and the boys kept using, but he could tell from their excitement that *camping* was a good thing – and he was eager to be part of it. With any luck *camping* might turn out to be a new game involving squirrels and smelly old bones.

Jack was getting into the idea now too. Setting up camp on Gulliver's Island would be like having their own private kingdom. He pictured himself striding around surveying his territory, building a fort and repelling all invaders. And he was sure that he'd be able to stow away a few extra snacks without Emily noticing. He started pedalling and zoomed ahead.

'What are we waiting for?' he shouted over his shoulder. 'Let's get packing!'

But next morning, as he munched on his bacon sandwich in the kitchen at Stone Cottage, Jack was feeling a lot less upbeat. He mooched into the living room to find Scott sprawling on the sofa in his dressing gown, half-heartedly dangling a piece of string for Boomerang – the tabby kitten that Aunt Kate had recently adopted – to play with.

Aunt Kate had said no to the camping trip.

Or at least she'd said she'd have to think about it. But Jack knew that when adults started *thinking* about things, they rarely had the thoughts you wanted them to have.

'I don't like to spoil your fun,' Aunt Kate had said, 'but spending several nights on an uninhabited island without even a tent could be dangerous.' She'd promised to phone and discuss it with the boys' father – who was away on an archaeological dig in Cambodia for the summer – but Jack was quite sure Dad would just leave the decision to Aunt Kate.

And when Emily turned up a few minutes later the news didn't get any better. Her parents had vetoed the solo camping trip idea, too.

'Dad offered to come and camp with us at a "nice campsite near Carrickstowe" instead,' she grumbled. 'But what's the point in that? Why do my parents always have to treat me like a *baby*?'

Emily knew she was being unfair; Maria and Seth Wild were some of the most laid-back parents on the planet, but she'd been so looking forward to the trip – and putting into practice all the wilderness survival techniques she'd read about – that Emily didn't care about minor details like fairness. In fact, for the first time since Jack and Scott had known her, she was in a full-scale, take-no-prisoners sulk. She threw herself down on a footstool, folded her arms and scowled at the vase of poppies on the dresser.

'Well, that's it! We *can't* go camping. We *haven't* got an investigation. We might just as well sit here and *vegetate* for the rest of the summer!'

Even Drift resting his head on Emily's knee and gazing up at her with his melting brown eyes couldn't console her.

Even Boomerang batting Drift's ears with her little velvet paws until he let her pounce on his tail couldn't make Emily laugh.

Jack and Scott looked at each other in despair. They were in uncharted territory. They had no idea how to tackle a Seriously Moping Emily.

Things hadn't improved by the next day. Emily was still ensconced on the footstool like a bad-tempered garden gnome, having only gone home to The Lighthouse to sleep. Scott lay on the sofa and refused to look up from a game of Total Strategy on his laptop.

Jack was relieved when the doorbell rang. At last, *something* might break up the gloom fest.

But his relief didn't last for long.

Aunt Kate hurried into the room wiping floury hands on her blue-striped apron. 'It's the police,' she said. 'They want to talk to you three.' She pinned a wisp of white hair back into its hairgrip and shook her head. 'What sort of trouble have you got yourselves into *this* time?'

Three

A Matter of Grave Concern

Trouble? Jack thought. Chance would be a fine thing! He'd spent the last twenty-four hours trying to jolly Emily out of her world-record attempt for the Longest Sulk in History. The only *trouble* he'd come close to was knocking a china elephant off the mantelpiece with the cushion he'd been using to wallop Scott when he'd threatened to gag Jack with an old sock if he told any more bad jokes. And the chip in its trunk was hardly even noticeable!

'Police?' Emily asked, with the first glimmer of interest she'd shown all day.

Two police officers followed Aunt Kate into the room. The first stepped forwards and removed her bowler hat to reveal dark hair slicked into a bun. 'PC Patel,' she said, flashing an identity card. 'This is PC Kennedy.' The pale freckled man beside her acknowledged his name with a bounce of his startlingly red eyebrows.

PC Patel swept her eyes like a searchlight from Jack to Scott to Emily to Drift and then back to Jack. She gave a curt nod as if all the evidence confirmed her worst suspicions. She glanced at the television and Scott reached out and turned it off. *The Simpsons* soundtrack was replaced by an uncomfortable silence broken only by Boomerang purring on the hearthrug.

'We are here on a matter of grave concern,' PC Patel stated at last. 'There has been a serious incident overnight . . .'

Jack was sure he hadn't done anything wrong – for once – and yet he couldn't help doubting himself. Had he committed some terrible abomination without knowing it? Could he have turned into a werewolf and roamed the island wreaking untold carnage during the hours of darkness? But it hadn't even been a full moon! He glanced at Scott, gulping nervously at the other end of the sofa. There was only one person in the room looking at all cheerful. Emily *always* perked up at the mention of serious crime.

'What sort of incident?' she asked.

PC Patel cleared her throat. 'A boy has gone missing.'

'Who?' Emily asked, round-eyed with curiosity. 'Where? When did this happen?'

PC Patel didn't answer. She took her time sitting down and blowing on the cup of tea that Aunt Kate had handed her. PC Kennedy stirred two spoons of sugar into his mug. Scott, Jack and Emily all held their breath, waiting for the details. PC Patel took a sip of her tea. 'I'm afraid I'm not at liberty to give out further information at this stage.'

'But why is it anything to do with us?' Scott asked reasonably.

PC Patel placed her cup on the coffee table. 'You were seen in the area.'

'What area?' Emily was almost exploding with impatience.

'Bosgoose Wood,' PC Kennedy said. PC Patel shot him a warning look, as if he'd leaked top-secret information to the enemy.

'Bosgoose Wood?' Jack echoed. Hairs stood up on the back of his neck as he remembered Emily's story about the old Hansel and Gretel lady in the tumbledown cottage. She was supposed to steal children, and now a boy had gone missing! But that woman had been dead for more than fifty years . . . *or had she*?

27

Jack's feverish thoughts were interrupted by Emily leaping up from the stool. 'Oh, I know! It's one of the boys from the school camp, isn't it? That teacher saw us watching from the trees.'

PC Patel stood up and brushed imaginary crumbs from her trousers. 'We'd like you to come along to the police station and help with our enquiries.'

'Are we under arrest?' Jack asked.

PC Patel managed a thin smile. 'Of course not. You're potential witnesses. You may have seen something relevant to the case. We need to take a statement from each of you separately so you don't influence each other.' She turned to Aunt Kate. 'Miss Trelawney, as their guardian, you'll need to accompany the boys. We've sent another car to pick up Miss Wild's father...'

⸺

Emily gazed around the dingy interview room. The beige walls were scuffed, her metal chair had a rickety leg and the surface of the table was pocked and gouged like an old school desk. The air was thick with stale coffee and sweat. Across the table, PC Patel was riffling through a file of papers, while a second officer Emily didn't recognize fiddled with the controls on the voice recorder.

'Now, there's nothing to worry about,' PC Patel began.

Emily smiled. She wasn't worried in the slightest.

She was having a lovely time. She was trying to figure out the precise nature of the police investigation. The missing boy wasn't a little kid. He was at least sixteen and he'd only been gone a few hours, but the police clearly already suspected foul play. They certainly weren't acting as if they thought he'd just sneaked out of camp for a wild night out in Carrickstowe. Judging from the upmarket camping kit, Braithwaite School was an elite private school, which meant the boy almost certainly came from a wealthy family. That could explain why PC Patel was being so cagey about giving out information. She hadn't even told Emily the boy's name. Were his parents celebrities trying to keep this out of the papers?

'Can you tell us what you saw at the school camp on Monday?' PC Patel asked.

At her side, Emily's dad leaned back in his chair and gave her an encouraging smile. The two police officers waited expectantly. *Aren't they even going to play Good Cop, Bad Cop?* Emily wondered. *Or wire me up to a lie-detector machine?* Didn't they know *anything* about interrogating a suspect?

Emily prided herself on her powers of observation and she couldn't resist showing off just the teensiest bit. She recounted the exact time she'd been in the woods, the weather conditions and the location of her observation post in the beech tree in relation to the position of the camp (including map co-ordinates).

She recited the registration numbers of the five jeeps, a complete list of each piece of equipment that had been unpacked and a detailed description of the three boys with the football and of the angry teacher.

In fact, she went on for so long that eventually PC Patel rested her chin in her hands and closed her eyes. Emily seized her chance and peeked at the folder on the table, doing her best to read upside down. PC Patel woke up and snatched the file back, but not before Emily had seen a name: *Sam Chambers.* Followed by the words HIGHLY SENSITIVE in red capitals.

Highly sensitive? Emily was turning the intriguing phrase over in her mind when the door was opened by a burly man in a perfectly pressed cream suit.

Emily recognized Detective Inspector Hassan. 'Have you questioned the other boys at the camp yet?' she asked eagerly. 'Did any of them see anything? What about forensics?'

D. I. Hassan held up both hands to stem the flood of questions. Then he smoothed down his glossy black moustache. 'We have it all under control, thank you, Emily.'

'You know these kids then?' PC Patel asked.

'We've assisted D. I. Hassan on several previous cases,' Emily told her stiffly.

D. I. Hassan's moustache twitched but he didn't say a word.

Meanwhile, in the next-door interview room, PC

Kennedy was showing Scott a photograph. Grey eyes gazed out of the picture from beneath a shaggy brown fringe.

Scott nodded. 'He's one of the boys we saw at the camp.'

'What can you tell me about him?' PC Kennedy asked.

Scott grinned. 'I wouldn't mind having him on my school football team.'

Moments later, Jack took Scott's place. PC Kennedy showed him the same photograph. 'Anything you remember about him?'

Jack squirmed in his chair. There *was* one thing. He hadn't mentioned it to Scott and Emily at the time because he'd only caught a glimpse, and it had seemed so odd he'd thought he might even have imagined it.

'Any detail. However small?' PC Kennedy prompted.

Jack made up his mind. 'He had a mouse in his pocket.'

PC Kennedy's fiery eyebrows shot up like a pair of caterpillars on a trampoline. 'A *mouse?*'

'Yeah, at least I think he did. A little white one. It peeked out of the pocket of his polo shirt when they were playing football. It was only for a second. It could have been a handkerchief, I suppose . . .'

PC Kennedy's eyebrows were in danger of going into orbit. He exchanged glances with the other police officer. 'Okaaaaay,' he murmured, tapping his pen on the table. 'I think that's enough for now.'

I knew I should've kept my mouth shut, Jack thought. Now the police had him down as a crazed loon or a compulsive liar – or both! He'd probably find an appointment letter for a therapist waiting for him when he got home.

———

D. I. Hassan escorted the friends – plus Emily's dad and Aunt Kate – out of the police station. 'We're trying to keep this lad's disappearance low-key for the time being,' he explained. 'We don't want to spread alarm. He's probably just wandered off and got lost.' The detective inspector looked sternly at Emily, Scott and Jack. 'And if you're thinking of going out searching for him, think again, do you hear me?'

Jack suppressed a smile. He'd be prepared to bet his last jelly baby that that was *exactly* what Emily had been thinking of.

'Of course we won't,' Emily said sweetly.

Jack did a double take.

She didn't even have her fingers crossed behind her back!

Four

Who is Sam Chambers?

As soon as the police car dropped the friends back at Stone Cottage they made straight for the treehouse in the back garden – pausing only to collect Drift, who'd been waiting patiently for them in the cottage. Drift was hoisted up in his special basket, doing his best to ignore Boomerang, who was scampering up the trunk of the mighty chestnut tree and shooting him *Cats Rule, Dogs Drool* looks as she passed.

Emily settled down on a cushion and took her notebook from the investigation kit she always carried in her large black shoulder bag. She turned to a new page and wrote OPERATION MISSING BOY. Then she added Name: Sam Chambers.

'They gave you his name?' Scott asked, looking over her shoulder.

'Not gave exactly,' Emily said. 'Let's just say I obtained certain information during the course of the interview.' She then wrote the words Highly Sensitive and circled them in red.

Jack looked up from prising the lid off the biscuit tin that he'd brilliantly thought to bring with him. Being interrogated by the police was hungry work. 'Highly sensitive!' he laughed. 'You mean he writes soppy love poems and cries at the sad bits in Bambi?' At that moment the lid flew off the tin, firing peanut-butter cookies all over the treehouse.

Scott caught one as it whizzed past his ear. 'It's the case that's sensitive, you dingbat, not the boy.'

Emily extracted a cookie from her notebook and fed it to Drift. 'That's right. They're trying to keep this disappearance hush-hush. But why? Who is Sam Chambers? And what could have happened to him? We don't have much to go on.'

Jack was tempted to mention the white mouse, but then he remembered PC Kennedy's eyebrows. Scott and Emily would probably fall out of the treehouse laughing.

Emily looked up from her notes. 'Now, where shall we start this investigation?'

'Aren't you forgetting something?' Jack asked.

'Oh, yes, thanks.' Emily took out her ruler and underscored *OPERATION MISSING BOY* with two neat lines.

'Not that!' Jack said. 'D. I. Hassan warned us not to go looking for the boy.'

'Exactly,' Emily said. 'Which is why we're *not* going looking for him. But D. I. Hassan didn't say *anything* about not asking a few questions, did he? Someone must have seen something.'

Scott thought for a moment. He didn't want to hamper the police investigation but, like Emily, he was eager to find out what had happened to the boy. 'We'll just have to use all our undercover skills so we don't arouse suspicion.'

But he needn't have worried. Castle Key was the kind of place you couldn't miss a dentist's appointment without everyone knowing about it. So, what with the Search and Rescue helicopters swooping overhead, motor boats chugging out from the harbour carrying teams of police divers, sniffer-dog handlers fanning out across the moors with their German Shepherds straining on their leads, and the school camp being cordoned off with bright orange crime-scene tape, the missing boy was already the main topic of conversation on the island.

When Jack, Scott and Emily called in at the mini-market later that afternoon to conduct their enquiries they found Mrs McElroy at the photocopier behind the Post Office counter, running off hundreds of posters with the words, MISSING SCHOOLBOY! HAVE YOU SEEN HIM? above a photo – which she'd somehow managed to acquire from one of the police officers on duty.

'Such a shame. He's a lovely boy,' Mrs McElroy said, handing Colin Warnock, the curate, a bundle of posters to paste up in the village.

Emily looked up from pretending to study the chewing-gum display. 'You knew him?' she asked. She couldn't believe that their intelligence gathering was getting off to such a flying start. She hadn't even asked a question yet!

Mrs McElroy started another batch of posters running. 'There was a bunch of those lads from the school camp in here on Monday afternoon. All messing about, buying sweets and cans of pop. This boy . . .' Mrs McElroy peered through her bifocal glasses at the photo on the poster, '. . . was the only one who was interested in the island. We had a nice little chat and he even bought a copy of *Discover Castle Key*.' She pointed to a rack of guidebooks next to the counter.

Discover Castle Key featured photographs of scenery and hearty people in walking boots on the front cover. *Dead boring*, Jack thought. *This Sam Chambers must be a real swot if he's more interested in reading a guidebook than stocking up on supplies for a midnight feast.*

But after their promising start, the friends didn't make much progress. Everyone had a theory about what had happened to the missing boy – some said he must have fallen down an old mine shaft, while others believed he'd simply got tired of camping and caught a bus home. Romantic types insisted that there was bound to be a girl involved, while those of a superstitious nature blamed aliens or restless spirits rising up from the ancient burial sites on the moors.

There were plenty of rumours, but not a shred of evidence.

When Emily arrived home that evening, Mum and Dad were busy preparing dinner for the new guests who had arrived at The Lighthouse – which they ran as a Bed and Breakfast – earlier that afternoon.

'A very nice group from Germany,' Mum told her. 'They've come to do some fishing.'

After their meal the German group sat in the big circular guest lounge on the ground floor, a sunny room full of squashy sofas and Emily's mum's vibrant paintings. Of the two men, Nico was huge with Incredible Hulk muscles and white-blond hair, while Rudi was equally tall but dark and wiry. There was also a woman, Anya, with the tanned, athletic look of a top-level tennis player. In their matching hiking shorts and squeaky-clean t-shirts, they looked like an advert for something wholesome like muesli or low-fat yoghurt. They were playing Scrabble and invited Emily to join them. Emily loved Scrabble – she'd memorized all the best words with Xs and Zs in them – and she couldn't resist. She won three games in a row, then made her excuses and said goodnight.

She snuggled into bed – Drift curled up on her feet – and read through her day's notes. She fell asleep thinking about the footballing boy with the floppy brown hair. *Who was he?* Scott had searched the internet for a famous politician or celebrity with a teenage son called Sam Chambers but had found nothing. More importantly, *where* was he? Wherever he was, Emily hoped he was safe.

She woke several hours later, with an annoying thought buzzing around her head like a trapped wasp. She'd left her mobile phone downstairs on the coffee table. It would be useless tomorrow if she didn't plug it into the charger. There were a lot of good points about having your bedroom on the eighth floor of a lighthouse – you could see for miles in all directions, for a start – but it had its downsides too, like the one hundred and twenty steps to the ground floor. Maybe she'd just go back to sleep and not bother. But, she reminded herself, a phone was vital for co-ordinating manoeuvres with

Jack and Scott when they were out on field ops. Would a true secret agent go out on a mission without the appropriate equipment just because she couldn't get out of bed? Of course not!

Emily padded down the spiral staircase with Drift at her heels.

She didn't switch on the light. She knew the guest lounge well enough to weave her way between the sofas and tables and lamps in the dark. She had just slipped her phone into her dressing-gown pocket when she noticed a ribbon of light beneath the closed door to the dining room. Someone must have left a lamp on. Emily was crossing to the door to do her bit for the environment and turn it off when she stopped dead in her tracks. A low mumble of voices was coming from behind the door. She glanced at the clock on the wall. It was almost three o'clock. Who was up at this time of night?

Emily tiptoed closer, knelt and placed one eye to the keyhole.

Rudi, Nico and Anya were huddled round a table. Surely they weren't *still* playing a marathon Scrabble match? Emily shifted position for a better view. No, they were looking at maps. Maybe they were planning their day's fishing?

She strained her ears but she couldn't catch what they were saying. Of course, they would be speaking German! Emily had been learning German at school and was disappointed she couldn't understand anything they were saying, apart from some names. *Sebastian . . . Orlando . . . Ferdinand.* It sounded like they were gossiping about their friends back home.

Emily was about to leave them to their late night chat when Drift – who was sitting next to her patiently waiting to get back to a really good dream about chasing giant rabbits – sighed softly. Through the keyhole Emily saw Anya snap her head up, her long dark ponytail swinging over her shoulder, and hold up a hand to silence the others. She turned to Nico, pointed to her eyes and then to the door – gesturing for him to check it out, just as Emily had seen undercover agents do in spy films. Nico nodded once and reached for a small black object that was lying on the table.

Is it a phone? Emily wondered. *Or a walkie-talkie?*

Then she stopped wondering and fled for the stairs.

Nico had picked up a gun!

Five

No Ordinary Fishing Trip

'At three o'clock in the morning?' Jack echoed. 'And they had guns?'

The sun was barely above the horizon when Emily had texted the boys to call an emergency meeting on the promontory near The Lighthouse. She'd refused to meet *inside* The Lighthouse for fear of being overheard by the 'German Gang', as she now insisted on calling them. She was convinced that the 'fishing holiday' was just a cover story. A cover story for *what* exactly, she hadn't yet figured out. But you didn't guard a room at gunpoint if you were just planning a fishing trip! Luckily Emily and Drift had made it to the stairs before Nico had spotted them last night.

'Are you sure you didn't dream it?' Scott asked as they sat down on the rocks at the end of the promontory and gazed across Key Bay. Sunlight was bouncing off the pale morning mist and the brightly coloured fishing boats in the harbour glittered in the haze. Scott shielded his eyes against the glare and yawned.

With Scott and Jack both doubting her story, Emily was almost starting to believe that she *had* dreamed the whole thing. *Almost*, but not quite! She had concrete evidence. She clicked onto the Recent History menu on her phone and waved the screen at the boys. 'See? 3.17 a.m. That's the time I plugged my phone in to the charger – which proves I went downstairs to fetch it in the middle of the night.'

Jack shrugged and watched Drift chasing seagulls. 'OK, so they were up late. Perhaps they had jet lag.'

'Jet lag!' Emily scoffed. 'They're only one hour ahead in Germany.' She shook her head and dropped her voice to a whisper, as if her words could carry over the crashing of the waves and the wailing of the gulls and penetrate the thick stone walls of The Lighthouse. 'No, I'm sure the German Gang has something to do with the missing boy.'

'On what evidence?' Scott demanded.

Emily sighed as if the answer should be obvious to anyone out of pre-school. 'A boy disappears. Two days later, a gang of gun-toting strangers turns up!'

'That's just the point,' Scott said, distinctly unimpressed at having been woken at the crack of dawn for this. '*Two days later!* If they wanted to kidnap Sam Chambers, they've missed the boat. He's already gone.'

Emily didn't like to admit it, but Scott had put his finger on the fatal flaw in her theory. Why had the German Gang come back if they'd already nabbed Sam Chambers?

'Ooh, I know, they're serial kidnappers, back to kidnap *another* boy!' Jack suggested. He pretended to look around in fear. 'Hey, I could be their next target!'

Scott muttered something that sounded suspiciously like, 'No such luck!' Then he turned to Emily. 'So what's this dangerous criminal gang doing now?'

'Eating breakfast,' Emily said flatly. To her disappointment the German Gang had been acting perfectly normally all morning.

Jack glanced longingly at The Lighthouse. Emily's message had been so urgent he'd only had time to snatch a slice of toast. 'Why don't I go and do a stake-out?' he offered. 'See what they're up to.'

'Stake-out? A *pig out*, more like,' Scott muttered.

When Jack returned a few moments later, there were telltale traces of fried egg on his chin.

'Situation Report!' Emily commanded.

Jack shrugged. 'They were asking your dad where they could hire a fishing boat.'

'Oh, yeah!' Emily snorted. 'Like we're meant to believe they're *really* going fishing! Well, we'll follow them and catch them out.'

'Will we?' Scott groaned. He'd been secretly hoping that the next mission would involve going back to bed for a couple of hours.

It wasn't long before Rudi, Nico and Anya emerged from The Lighthouse. They headed along the promontory and took the winding path down to the harbour, unaware that they were being tailed.

Jack, Scott, Emily and Drift established an Observation Post behind a stack of crates near the harbour wall and watched as the German Gang approached a man unloading a catch of sole and pollack on the quayside. When he looked up, they saw that it was their friend Old Bob. As always, he was wearing his ancient blue cable-knit jumper and woollen cap even though the sun had now burned off the sea mist and the heat was already building.

Old Bob walked the German Gang along the jetty to a sparkling white catamaran called *Double Trouble*. A burly man appeared on deck, a boat hook in one hand and a coffee mug in the other. Scott recognized Jago Merrick, a fisherman who moored several boats in Castle Key harbour. Merrick beckoned the German Gang aboard and began showing them around and pointing out the fishing tackle stowed on the deck.

Twenty minutes later, the engine started. Ropes were freed from the mooring rings, the gangplank was pulled up, the anchor was raised and *Double Trouble* was off. Old Bob and Jago Merrick stood on the jetty, squinting into the sun as they watched her nosing out into the bay.

Scott looked at Jack. Surely *now* Emily would believe that the German Gang really was going fishing!

'That's odd,' Emily mumbled. 'They've not taken Jago!' And before the boys could ask what she meant, she was running off along the jetty.

Old Bob – who was now swabbing down his boat, *Morwenna* – stooped to ruffle Drift's ears. 'What're you kids up to this fine day then?'

'Oh, not much,' Emily said quickly. 'Where were those people going? The ones who just hired *Double Trouble*?'

'They're staying at The Lighthouse and Em's mum was wondering what time they'd be back for their evening meal,' Scott improvised, trying to cover up for Emily's blatant nosiness.

Old Bob looked up from unreeling a hosepipe. He knew the friends well enough to know that they were probably up to something. But he also knew them well enough to know that it was best not to ask. 'They've gone to Pirate Cove for the day, wreck-fishing,' he shouted over the jet of water he was spraying on the deck. 'They're after the big conger eels and ling mainly. I caught a fifty-pounder over there myself the other week!'

'But don't fishing parties always charter a skipper along with the boat – someone local who knows all the best spots?' Emily asked.

Old Bob shrugged. 'They usually do. But this lot just wanted the boat. They've all got their Yachtmasters' certificates so they're qualified. And,' he added with a wink, 'they paid Jago up-front in cash.' As the old fisherman turned to stare after *Double Trouble*, he caught Drift and Jack in the hose spray. They both yelped in surprise.

'Satisfied now?' Jack asked Emily as they walked back along the harbour. He was still wringing water out of his t-shirt. 'The only thing the German Gang's going to be kidnapping is a conger eel or two!'

But Emily shook her head. 'I still think it's a cover story. Let's take *Gemini* and follow them to Pirate Cove.'

Jack stopped. 'No way. I'm not rowing all the way to Pirate Cove in this heat to *watch people fishing*.' Jack wasn't a fan of fishing; he didn't have the patience for it. Watching other people fishing sounded even worse!

Emily grinned. 'You don't have to. The outboard

motor is still attached from when Dad took some guests on a trip to Westward Beach.'

Jack and Scott gave up. There was simply no point arguing with Emily when she had one of her ideas.

———

The friends moored in a tiny inlet not far from Pirate Cove where they could spy on *Double Trouble* from behind the rocks. Jack took first turn with the binoculars. Not that there was anything to see. *Double Trouble* dropped anchor above the wreck of the *Mermaid* and Rudi, Anya and Nico sat around holding their fishing rods. There was a flurry of activity as Anya caught a small eel. The two men took photographs of her holding it up and then threw it back over the side.

Half an hour later, two more eels had been caught and returned to the sea. Scott had threatened to throw Jack overboard too if he uttered the word 'boring' one more time, and even Drift was fed up with barking at seagulls.

'We'll give it another half hour . . . then we'll go . . .' Emily agreed at last.

'Hallelujah!' Jack cried.

'Shut up!' Scott hissed.

'No need to snap!' Jack snapped.

'No,' Scott said. 'I mean shut up and *listen*! They're on the move!'

Scott was right. *Double Trouble*'s motor was growling into life. The catamaran left Pirate Cove and disappeared round the south-eastern tip of the island.

Jack laughed. 'They obviously couldn't stand the excitement any more either.'

'Maybe they're looking for another wreck to fish?' Scott suggested.

Emily shook her head. 'There aren't any wrecks along the east coast. Jago will have told them that. No, they're up to something.'

Scott tugged the starter cord on the motor. 'Well, there's only one way to find out.'

Double Trouble sped northwards along the east coast of Castle Key island, carving a double track of frothy white water in its wake. *Gemini* followed at a distance. With plenty of other boats out on the water, Emily hoped the German Gang wouldn't notice they had a stalker. Just when she thought the catamaran was going to cruise all the way to mainland Cornwall, it changed course and began to head inland.

Emily surveyed the rugged coastline through the binoculars. 'I knew it! They're making for Chicken Bay!' she breathed.

'So?' Jack asked.

But Scott understood what Emily meant. 'The Braithwaite School campsite is just up there, isn't it?' He pointed towards the cliffs that ringed the small bay.

'We're right below the place where Sam Chambers went missing.'

Emily grinned. '*Now* do you believe this is no ordinary fishing trip?'

Six

Crossing the Abyss

Chicken Bay – named for the hen-shaped rock formation halfway up the cliff face – was teeming with activity. A coastguard boat and two police launches were patrolling. Red and white buoys bobbed in the waves to mark the spots where teams of scuba divers were searching the water. Scott tried not to let his eyes stray to the jagged rocks that pierced the swirling waters. If Sam Chambers had fallen off the cliffs there was little hope of finding him alive.

He watched through the binoculars as *Double Trouble* stopped short of the bay and dropped anchor in a small cove. Moments later, Anya and Nico jumped from the back of the catamaran, swam ashore and began to climb the path that snaked up to the cliff top.

'Come on! Let's see what they're doing!' Jack urged.

'I think they might notice if we start following them up that path,' Scott pointed out. He swept the binoculars along the coastline, stopping suddenly as something caught his eye. He zoomed in. There was a second – steeper – path not far from their current position. 'Funny,' he muttered. 'That path only seems to start halfway up the cliff . . .'

Emily took the binoculars. 'No, it starts from a tiny inlet. It's tucked so far behind those massive rocks that you can't see it from the sea. That's why it's called Forgotten Cove.'

Scott grabbed the tiller and swung *Gemini* round. Then he revved up the motor and accelerated so fast the bow reared up out of the waves.

Jack clung to the sides of the boat. 'Whoah! What are you doing?'

'Going to Forgotten Cove!' Scott shouted over the engine roar. 'Drop me off there and I'll climb that path and see what Anya and Nico are up to on the clifftop.'

'I'm coming with you!' Jack yelled.

Emily was about to say she'd join them when she

remembered Drift. She wasn't sure he'd make it up the cliff path. And, anyway, someone had to keep an eye on Rudi in *Double Trouble*. 'We'll take *Gemini* back and meet you at Bosgoose Cottage,' she told the boys.

Scott and Jack each grabbed a water bottle, then they slid over the side of the little boat and waded ashore.

Jack stopped to take a swig of water. He felt as if someone had replaced his calf muscles with wet concrete. The cliff path was even steeper than it had looked from the boat. It wasn't technically difficult (that would at least have made it interesting!) just hard work – like a never-ending flight of stairs.

Whose stupid idea was it to climb a cliff path in a heat wave anyway? *Oh, yes,* Jack thought, glaring at Scott a few paces ahead, a square of dark sweat gluing his t-shirt to his back. *I remember. I should've let him do this on his own.* Now Scott had stopped too. He was gripping the rickety handrail that had been screwed into the rock so tightly his fingers had turned white.

'You alright?' Jack called.

Do I look alright? Scott thought. He'd been doing fine, as long as he held onto the rail and didn't look down. They were nearly at the top now. But suddenly he'd come to a patch where the path had crumbled away in a mini-avalanche of loose shale and rubble.

The gap wasn't very wide. He only had to step over and he'd be on his way. That's what he told himself. Unfortunately, his brain didn't believe him. His brain saw a vast bottomless chasm. It saw Scott plunging headfirst into the abyss. It saw the rocks below rushing up to meet him.

Scott screwed his eyes closed and pressed himself against the rock face.

Jack caught up. He took one look at the eroded path and one look at the porridge-grey shade of his brother's face and knew Scott was in trouble. The long, long drop to the waves and rocks made Jack think of exciting adrenaline-pumping stuff like bungee jumping and skydiving and an awesome-looking thing he'd seen on TV where you leaped off a mountain and glided around in a flying-squirrel suit. It was clearly *not* having the same effect on Scott.

'It's OK,' Jack coaxed. 'It's a tiny little gap. Hold on to me and step over it.'

Scott shook his head without opening his eyes.

Jack felt the first flicker of fear. What if Scott fainted? He really could fall. But they couldn't hang around up here. The cliff face was collecting the sun's rays like a giant magnifying glass. They'd have sunstroke as well as vertigo to deal with soon.

Jack knew he had to take charge. He inched past Scott on the narrow path. Then, with his face to the cliff, he stretched one leg out across the void and felt for solid ground until he was straddling the gap with one foot on either side. Then he reached out his hand and grabbed the rail on the far side. With his free hand he gripped Scott by the elbow.

'Do exactly what I say and do it now!' Jack instructed. Scott gulped and clenched his jaw. Without giving him time to think, Jack pulled him to the edge of the gap. Scott had his back to the cliff face so that they were face to face in a tight embrace now. 'Lift your right foot and feel for the other side!' Jack barked into Scott's ear.

Wedged chest to chest with Jack, Scott had no choice but to obey orders. At last his foot found the other side. He felt along the cliff and his hand touched the hot metal of the rail. For a heart-stopping moment his foot slipped on a loose stone. His stomach lurched. But he was held firm by the force of Jack's body.

He grabbed hold of the handrail and pulled himself across.

When they finally reached the top, Scott crawled away from the cliff edge and lay on his stomach with his face in a tuft of heather, hugging the lovely flat horizontal surface. 'Cheers!' he said, reaching for the bottle of water Jack held out to him. He took a long swig. 'Cheers!' he repeated as he passed it back. He glanced back at the cliff edge and gave a tiny nod to signify that this single syllable of thanks covered the incident on the path as well as the water.

Jack grinned. 'Don't mention it, old boy!' But he stored it away in his memory, of course, ready for the next time Scott needed reminding just who was the most awesomely heroic of the Carter brothers.

Scott sat up and looked around to get his bearings. A little way inland the trees of Bosgoose Wood stood tall and dark, their leaves rustling as if whispering secrets to each other. The heath stretched away to the right. Snatches of music and the warning beeps of a reversing vehicle could be heard coming from the school camp, hidden in a dip behind a gentle rise of the land.

Suddenly two figures appeared over the edge of the cliff, silhouetted against the dazzling blue of the sky. It had to be Anya and Nico! They began to walk rapidly across the heath, heading straight for the school camp.

Scuttling from the cover of one stand of gorse bushes to the next, Scott and Jack followed. Next thing Jack knew, Scott had grabbed his arm and he was flying through the air and landing in a gorse bush. 'What was that for?' he gasped.

'Shh!' Scott hissed. 'There are two police officers coming up the track. We don't want them to see us here. You know what D. I. Hassan said about not looking for the boy.'

'Well, we're not, are we?' Jack grumbled, extracting gorse thorns from every millimetre of his anatomy.

'We're stalking boring German people who are only interested in eel fishing and hiking . . .'

'I'm not so sure about that. Look!' Scott whispered.

Jack peeped out through the screen of spiky branches studded with yellow flowers. The police officers had stopped a little way along the track, exactly where Anya and Nico had been standing just seconds earlier. 'Where've the Germans gone?' he asked.

Scott grinned. 'They dived into a gorse bush as well.'

'Why?' Jack asked, wincing as he pulled a thorn the size of a small bayonet out of his thigh. 'These bushes are lethal!'

'Same reason we did, I guess. They didn't want the police to see them. Which means . . .' Scott paused for Jack to fill in the end of the sentence.

Jack thought for a moment. 'Er, they're bank-robbers on the run from the law?'

Scott rolled his eyes. 'No! It means Emily was right. They're something to do with the missing boy!'

But Jack wasn't listening. He was staring at a spider the size of a tarantula creeping towards his foot. He shrank away, but the monster was almost upon him, homing in on the scent of blood from his thorn-scratches.

Scott peeked out from their hideout again. The police officers had moved on but Anya and Nico hadn't broken cover yet. He could hear the murmur of voices coming from the next clump of gorse. If he could just get close enough to hear what they were saying . . .

'Stay here!' he whispered to Jack.

'But . . . the *spider*!' Jack whimpered.

Scott took no notice. But then he remembered his wobbly moment on the cliff path. He scooped up the spider – which was hardly bigger than a full stop – and lobbed it gently into the undergrowth. Then he began tunnelling through the bracken. The dry fronds crackled and crunched around his ears. It was like trying to do a stealth raid with crisp packets strapped all over your body! He didn't dare creep any closer, but held his breath and listened. Dust from the dry bracken tickled his throat. A thorn in his trainer pricked at his heel. Somewhere a grasshopper was chirping.

Then the voices started again.

And now he could hear every word . . .

Seven

A Code of Some Sort

From deep inside the gorse bush Anya's voice was as rapid and urgent as gunfire. Nico made no reply. It sounded as if Anya was talking into a phone or radio. Scott cursed under his breath. He could *hear* the words but he couldn't understand them. She was speaking in German. He was about to give up when at last he heard *something* he recognized. *Golf!*

Scott's heart sank. Had he climbed a cliff, been ripped

to shreds by a gorse bush and commando-crawled through the undergrowth just to hear Anya shouting at someone about messing up her booking for a round of golf? Now she was repeating it, but this time in a list of random words: *Echo, Golf, Lima, Lima.* What was she on about? Lima was the capital city of Peru! Surely she wasn't going to play golf in South America. No, it had to be some kind of code.

'Lima,' Anya said again. 'Lima, Mike, Sierra, Hotel.'

Was she meeting someone called Mike at the Sierra Hotel in Lima?

Of course not! Scott only just stopped himself laughing out loud when he suddenly realized what all those strange words meant.

At that moment Nico and Anya crawled out of the bush. Scott burrowed deeper into the bracken, trying to make himself invisible, hoping they wouldn't hear the manic thumping of his heart. At last, when he was sure they had gone, he did a high-speed shuffle back through the bracken tunnel. 'Quick!' he told Jack. 'They're on the move again.'

But before the boys could follow, they heard footsteps. The police officers were back! Hunkered down under the gorse once more, the black material of a police uniform trouser leg just centimetres from their noses, Scott and Jack waited. When the officers had finally moved on, they popped their heads up like periscopes in a sea of bracken. Anya and Nico were nowhere to be seen.

'We've lost them,' Scott grumbled.

Jack stood up. 'Good. I've had enough of this! And next time you decide to rugby-tackle me into a spider-infested gorse bush, can you give me some warning? I'll make sure I'm wearing full body armour. I feel like a human pincushion!'

Scott grinned. 'You look like one. Come on, let's get to Bosgoose Cottage and wait for Emily.'

By the time they reached the old cottage Jack had cheered up. It was cool in the woods after being chargrilled on the cliff. And then there were the emergency supplies he'd so cleverly thought to stash away – just in case they ever decided to use the place as their operations base. He reached behind the loose stone in the wall and pulled out a packet of shortbread – which looked as if it had been slightly nibbled by a small animal – and three Cokes. He passed one to Scott and glugged the other down in a single draught. He eyed the third can, but resisted manfully, and handed it to Emily when she arrived with Drift a few moments later.

The three friends made themselves comfortable on a grassy bank, leaning against the cottage wall, while Drift investigated the area around Jack's emergency 'supply cupboard' as if searching for crumbs. Scott and Jack recounted the story of how they had followed Anya and Nico across the heath from the top of the cliff. 'They seemed to be monitoring activity around the school camp,' Scott explained as Emily made notes in her notebook.

'Yeah, and you should have seen how fast they legged it into a gorse bush when the police came by,' Jack laughed. 'Highly suspicious!'

Emily looked up from writing. 'Rudi was just the same. After I dropped you guys at Forgotten Cove, I saw a coastguard boat coming out from the bay. Rudi didn't hang around to find out what they wanted. *Double Trouble* steamed straight back to Pirate Cove, full speed ahead! I get the feeling the German Gang has something to hide.'

'There's more,' Scott said. 'I overheard Anya talking on the phone. It was all in German of course but I picked out a few words.'

Emily leaned closer, her pen poised over her notebook. 'What did she say?'

'First thing I got was Echo, Golf, Lima, Lima,' Scott said.

'Sounds like a code of some sort,' Emily murmured.

'It took me a moment to work it out, too,' Scott said. 'They're the words you use to spell out letters so people don't muddle them up.'

Jack laughed. 'Like in all the action films.' He clamped his shortbread to his ear like a radio receiver. 'Come in, Tango Charlie Foxtrot. Do you read me?'

Emily nodded. 'Of course! It's the international spelling alphabet.' She was kicking herself for not recognizing it straight away. It was listed at the back of the *Survival Guide for Secret Agents* along with loads of other useful information that a special agent might need at her fingertips, and she'd learned it off by heart. 'Echo stands for E, Golf stands for G and Lima is L.'

'So that makes EGLL.' Jack turned to Scott. 'So, what does it mean, Einstein?'

Scott shrugged. 'Don't ask me. I'm just the ideas man! I'll leave the boring details to you lesser mortals.'

Jack flashed a look at his brother to remind him that if he got any *more* big-headed the little matter of the Chasm of Doom might just have to be mentioned . . .

'It could mean anything,' Scott said quickly. 'English Gnomes Like Lollipops?'

'What about Earwigs Gatecrash Ludicrous Library?' Jack suggested.

Meanwhile Emily was staring silently at her notebook. She wrote the initials *E.G.L.L.* in the middle of a page and circled them in red. She couldn't help feeling she'd seen that sequence of letters before.

Emily tried to rewind, to pinpoint the moment when the feeling of familiarity had first begun. It was definitely nothing to do with gnomes or lollipops or earwigs! No, it had been when she'd started thinking about the spelling alphabet being in the reference section of her book . . . yes, that was it . . . the key to the puzzle was concealed somewhere in those pages. She reached for her bag and pulled out the *Survival Guide for Secret Agents* – it was a hefty volume but she always carried it with her just in case. She flicked through to the back and began to scan the tables, lists and charts . . . Suddenly she saw it: *ICAO codes.* 'I've got it!' she shouted. 'It's airports. EGLL is London Heathrow!'

Scott shook his head. 'No way! The code for Heathrow is LHR.'

Emily smiled. It was the triumphant smile Jack recognized as the one teachers use when they ask a trick question like, *How many animals of each kind did Moses take on to the ark?* and you walk right into it by sticking your hand up and saying 'Two!' when the correct answer is zero because it was Noah who did the ark thing, not Moses, and everyone else in the class pretends *they* knew it all along.

'No!' she said. 'That's the International Air Transport Authority code. Those are ones that the public knows. But the International Civil Aviation Organization codes are the official ones used by air traffic control. They have four letters instead of three and they're organized by . . .'

Jack stretched back on the warm grass and let Emily's voice wash over him. He had to admit, it was impressive that she knew all this stuff but did she have to give them a lecture about it? Through half-closed eyes he watched through the cottage doorway. Drift was still scrabbling away at the base of the wall near the niche where the shortbread had been stored. He'd been fixated on the same spot for ages now.

'What's up, Drifty?' Jack called, as he got up and went in to have a look. 'You cornered a rabbit or something?'

There was nothing on the ground, so Jack pulled out the loose stone and groped around inside the gap. Suddenly his hand brushed against something soft.

He staggered back as if he'd been zapped by a stun gun. Raising a trembling finger, Jack pointed at the wall. '*Sam Chambers!*' he gasped.

Eight

The Most Interesting Clues Ever

*S*am Chambers?

Scott heard Jack's shriek and ran into the cottage with Emily. Jack had to be messing around! There was no way a sixteen-year-old boy could fit into that little hole in the wall. Unless, of course – ice-cold dread gripped Scott's gut – it was only a *part* of him in there.

Emily turned to Jack with a puzzled expression. 'There's nothing there!'

'I definitely saw it!' Jack insisted. Drift wagged his tail and licked Jack's knees as if to back up his story. 'So did Drift!'

'Saw *what*?' Scott was starting to suspect that this was one of Jack's lame pranks. Something was bound to spring out on an elastic band and flick him on the nose when he looked in the hole. Well, he wasn't falling for it.

'The white mouse!' Jack said.

'You've been out in the sun too long, mate!' Scott laughed. 'Your brain's fried!' Then he clapped his hand to his forehead as if it suddenly all made sense. 'Of course,' he joked. '*That's* what happened. The old child-snatching witch-lady of Bosgoose Cottage put a spell on Sam Chambers and turned him into a white mouse.' He nudged Emily's elbow. 'When we find this mouse you should try kissing it and see if it turns into a prince.'

'That's *frogs*, not *mice*!' Emily pointed out. 'You really need to brush up on your fairy tales. And what would I want a prince for anyway?' But suddenly her voice faltered and she stared at the wall as if entranced. Drift, Jack and Scott followed her eyeline until all four stood gaping at the gap in the stonework.

A white mouse with bright pink eyes was sitting up on its back legs, its whiskers twitching as it nibbled delicately on a beechnut. The mouse looked up and regarded the visitors with an expression of mild interest, as if trying to recall whether it had met them before.

Jack grinned. 'Told you!' He held out his hand. The mouse hopped into his palm. 'You're the one who took a bite out of my shortbread, aren't you?'

Scott stared at Jack. 'OK, there *is* a white mouse. I'll give you that. But that doesn't even begin to explain why you yelled "Sam Chambers" at the top of your voice!'

'This is his mouse,' Jack explained in a matter-of-fact tone.

Emily laughed. 'How do you know?'

'Remember when we were in the tree watching the boys from the school camp playing football? I saw this little guy pop his nose out from Sam Chambers' pocket.'

Scott shook his head. 'And you didn't think to mention this because . . .'

'I only got a glimpse. I wasn't sure. I told PC Kennedy about it and he looked at me as if I'd started skipping around the room singing *Twinkle, Twinkle Little Star* with a pineapple on my head, so I thought I'd keep quiet after that . . .' Jack broke off and squealed with laughter as the mouse ran up inside his t-shirt, its sharp little claws tickling his skin.

'Ah, but how do you know it's the *same* mouse?' Emily asked seriously.

Scott did a double take. There were times when Emily was even loopier than Jack! 'Well, we *could* take a DNA sample and check its fingerprints,' he said, 'but how many other tame white mice do you think are running around on Castle Key?'

Emily grinned. 'Yeah, good point! But how did it get here?'

'Could it have found its way from the school camp?' Scott wondered.

Emily thought for a moment. 'Across the heath? It's unlikely. An owl or a fox would have picked it off within minutes.'

'Which means . . .' Scott said, all of a sudden realizing just how massive a clue this little mouse was.

'. . . Sam Chambers must have been here.' Emily finished Scott's sentence for him. She gazed around the abandoned room, with its rubble-strewn floor and weed-tangled walls. 'The police can't have connected this place with Sam's disappearance, otherwise they'd have sealed it off as a crime scene.'

'That's because they don't know about Boz!' Jack said.

'Boz?' Scott asked.

Jack looked down at the trusting pink-eyed gaze of the little mouse. 'I've named him Bosgoose. Boz for short. I'll look after him until Sam Chambers turns up.'

'Sorry,' Emily said. 'But that mouse is evidence. We'll have to hand him over to the police.'

Reluctantly Jack phoned the police station as soon as he arrived back at Stone Cottage. It was so unfair! Emily

70

had Drift and Scott had practically adopted Boomerang as his own – the little cat slept on his bed every night. So how come he wasn't even allowed a tiny, temporary mouse? But to his surprise and delight, D. I. Hassan said Jack could keep Boz for now.

'We'll send someone out to take some pictures of the mouse,' the detective inspector said. 'But I don't think we need to take it into custody. I'll trust you to look after it for us.'

Jack glowed with pride. 'Hello, pleased to meet you,' he introduced himself to an imaginary audience. 'Jack Carter here, Official Mouse-Warden to the Carrickstowe Constabulary.' He was taking his responsibilities seriously. He immediately set about constructing a cosy home for Boz out of an old shoebox, complete with shredded newspaper, water and a mixture of seeds and oats from Aunt Kate's pantry. The hardest part was going to be keeping Boz out of the clutches of Boomerang, but Jack made a solemn vow that he would protect his new charge with his very life! When – or *if* (although Jack didn't like to think the word *if* out loud) – Sam Chambers came back, he'd find his little friend in good hands.

Meanwhile, Emily had to return to The Lighthouse to help with the laundry. She found her mum in the kitchen behind the ironing board in a cloud of steam that stuck her dark curls to her face. She was smiling as if she'd bought Emily the most fabulous Christmas present ever and was bursting with the secret.

'You know that camping trip you're so keen to go on?'

Emily started folding tablecloths. 'Camping?' she asked. Then she remembered the trip that had seemed like the most important thing in the world only two days ago. She'd forgotten all about it since Operation Missing Boy had come along.

'Dad and I have had a talk about it. You can go to Black Rock Island over on the east coast. Old Bob is going to be doing some night fishing near there for the next few nights. He's agreed to keep an eye on you – but he won't interfere unless you radio him for help. The boys' Aunt Kate has agreed to it, so you can go tonight if you like.' She beamed at Emily as if expecting whoops of joy. 'Well?' she prompted, when Emily didn't respond. 'What do you say?'

Emily poked her head out of the duvet cover she was wrestling with. 'Thanks, Mum, that's great, but we're *way* too busy to go off camping now.'

'But I thought . . .' Maria Wild gave up and shook her head slowly as she ran the iron over a pillowcase. 'Kids!' she muttered. 'I'll never understand them . . .'

As soon as the last sheet hit the airing cupboard Emily hurried back to Stone Cottage. She found Jack lying on the lawn in the back garden trying to teach Boz to shake hands. Boomerang had been shut inside the cottage while the little mouse was on the loose and was sitting on the living room windowsill swishing her tail in furious indignation.

Scott was hunched over his laptop at the patio table. 'I've figured out some more of what Anya was talking about on the phone,' he said, as Emily pulled up a chair. 'We'd got as far as Echo Golf Lima Lima meaning Heathrow airport, before we were side-tracked by white mice . . .' He glanced at Jack, who was now setting up a mouse-sized obstacle course. 'But she also said Lima Mike Sierra Hotel. That's the spelling alphabet too.'

Emily gripped the table in excitement. 'LMSH? It sounds like another airport code. It's in Germany, isn't it? That's where Anya and her gang come from.'

'That's what I thought . . . at first,' Scott added, pausing to enjoy his dramatic moment. 'But I looked it up. It's not in Germany.' He angled the laptop screen towards Emily and pointed to a tiny dot on a map of Europe.

Emily screwed up her eyes to read the miniscule print. '*Medania?*'

Scott nodded. 'LMSH is the code for Saint Hortense Airport in Medania.'

Jack looked up from coaxing Boz to jump over a

stack of toilet rolls. 'No way. There's no such country as Medania!'

'Oh, yes, there is!' Scott fired back.

'Well, I've never heard of it!'

'That doesn't mean anything,' Scott laughed. 'You hadn't heard of *Denmark* until last week when I told you that that's where Danish pastries come from.'

Emily clicked on the information box on the map. '"Medania",' she read out. '"A tiny, vastly wealthy principality in the mountainous region between Italy and Slovenia. Ruler, King Orlando III. Official language, Medanian."' Emily looked up. 'No wonder I couldn't understand anything they were saying last night at The Lighthouse. They were speaking Medanian, not German!' She stared at the screen. Although she didn't know the first thing about Medania, *something* about it was ringing a bell. She read the text over and over again, trying to put her finger on it. Suddenly it came to her. 'King Orlando!' she cried. 'Orlando was one of the names I heard Anya and Rudi and Nico talking about. It can't be a coincidence that they've mentioned the airport *and* the king's name. The German Gang must be from Medania!'

Jack looked up from his mouse training. 'We'll have to give them a new name. How about the Medanian Mafia?'

Emily turned to a new page in her notebook and wrote the heading, *Clues*. Then she added:

(1) White mouse at Bosgoose Cottage
(2) Medania Saint Hortense Airport

Operation Missing Boy was turning out to be a truly baffling case. These were some of the most interesting clues ever, yet she had no idea what they meant. Why had Sam Chambers been to Bosgoose Cottage? And what did a missing schoolboy have to do with the three armed Medanian strangers who were sneaking around the island?

'Are you stuck?' Jack asked, noticing Emily staring at her notebook. 'You know what would help here?'

'What?' Emily asked hopefully. Was Jack about to come up with one of his rare but brilliant strokes of genius?

Jack grinned. 'A really enormous pizza!'

Nine

On the Right Track

'I've worked it all out,' Jack said, once they were settled at a window table in Dotty's Tea Rooms and he'd dealt with the serious business of ordering a Super-Special pizza with extra pepperoni and olives. 'The missing boy is from Medania.'

'*Sam Chambers* doesn't sound like a very Medanian name,' Emily pointed out, leafing through the *Teach Yourself Medanian* book she'd checked out of the library on the way to the café. She was determined to swot up on the language so she could understand what Rudi, Anya and Nico were plotting next time she had a chance to spy on them.

Scott stirred his Coke with a straw. 'It could be a false name. That would explain why I couldn't find anything about this Sam Chambers on the internet.'

'Precisely,' Jack said. 'Remember that thing about Medania being "vastly wealthy". Our Sam must be the son of some mega-loaded banker or business tycoon. I bet he's been kidnapped for an enormous ransom, like ten million pounds . . . All that talk about airports, they're probably planning how they'll transport him back to Medania once the ransom has been paid— Ah, thank you,' he interrupted himself, as Dotty placed a pizza the size of a satellite dish in front of him. He grinned up at Scott and Emily as he dolloped ketchup all over it. 'You're speechless with admiration, I know. First I think of pizza, then the solution to the mystery. Two brainwaves for the price of one!'

'Do you *have* to talk with your mouth full?' Scott grumbled. 'It's revolting!'

My genius is wasted on these people! Jack thought. He opened his mouth even wider and chewed with extra gusto just to wind his brother up. He was offering a morsel of mozzarella to Boz, who was peeping out from his t-shirt sleeve, when he noticed that Emily was pointing at her eyes, and then, very surreptitiously, towards the door. Why couldn't she just say 'look over there'? Jack wondered.

Jack looked across to see two teenaged boys hurrying into the café. Both had the hoods of their hoodies pulled up to hide their faces. They glanced around the room and then back over their shoulders. *They seriously need to improve their shoplifting technique*, Jack thought. They might as well have been handing out leaflets that said they were planning to snatch money from the till or raid the cake counter.

The hooded boys both jumped as the bell on the door jangled behind them. Then they crossed the café. But to Jack's surprise, they didn't try to make off with pockets full of pilfered pastries. Instead they sidled up to the counter and asked for menus before sitting down at a table in the back corner.

'It's the boys from the school camp,' Scott whispered. 'The ones who were playing football with Sam Chambers.'

Emily's face lit up. 'Result! We just need an excuse to talk to them. They could have vital information.'

But Jack had stopped listening. He'd seen something through the window that required emergency action. The barrel-shaped teacher with the sergeant-major moustache was on the seafront outside and the way he was storming along, his face and bald head the colour of raw steak, he wasn't just out for a leisurely stroll. Jack was an expert in the art of evading teacher surveillance; he had, for example, frequently spun out the delivery of a note to the school office for an entire double maths lesson. He grabbed the red checked curtains and yanked them closed, just as the teacher stooped to peer in through the window, shading his eyes against the sun. Then Jack shot across the café, grabbed the two boys by the arms and bundled them – and himself – through a door marked *Staff Only*.

Only just in time! The door crashed open and the sergeant major strode to the counter. 'You seen two of my lads in here? One black, one white?' He barked to Dotty. 'Both in deep doo-doo when I catch them.'

Dotty turned round from sliding pizzas into the oven. 'Yes, they're . . .' She looked over to the corner table. 'Oh, they've gone. Hey, Scott! Emily!' she called. 'Did you see where those boys went?'

Scott shrugged. 'I think they left.'

'Ages ago,' Emily agreed.

Dotty frowned at the window. 'Why're the curtains closed?'

'Er, the sun was in my eyes,' Emily said quickly. 'I think I'm getting a migraine.'

Satisfied that the boys were no longer on the premises, the sergeant major departed, slamming the door behind him.

Scott knocked on the door of the storeroom. 'Coast's clear! You can come out now.' He and Emily had, of course, figured out what Jack was up to as soon as the teacher had walked in.

'Oh, there you are,' Dotty said, as the teenagers trooped back to their table.

'They were just, er, looking for the bathroom,' Jack said. 'Got a bit lost.'

Already firm friends with the two teenagers, Jack pulled up a chair at their table. He beckoned for Scott, Emily and Drift to join them too and began to make the introductions. 'This is Harry,' he said, indicating a sporty-looking boy with a blond quiff and sunburn on his freckled nose.

'And I'm Jamal,' the other boy said, waving his fork in greeting. 'Awesome pizza! Thanks for the rescue mission back there,' he added, touching knuckles with Jack.

'Yeah, cheers, we'd have been dead meat if Mr Rodman had caught us.' Harry mimed a throat-slitting action. 'We're not meant to leave the camp while the police are still investigating the . . .' He hesitated. 'Well, you know. But we were getting cabin fever.'

Jamal nodded. 'The Rodmanator is our PE teacher. He used to be in the army and I don't think anyone's told him he's left. He's all about discipline with a Capital D!'

'And polishing things,' Harry chipped in. 'Boots, trophies, desks. You name it, he makes us polish it "until I can see my face in it",' Harry mimicked the teacher's gruff voice.

Jamal grimaced. 'If I had an ugly mug like his I wouldn't be so keen on seeing it all the time!'

Jack roared with laughter. He'd thought the boys from the swanky school would be stuck-up, but they were dead normal. Not to mention the fact that they'd offered to buy ice creams all round as a thank you for saving their skins!

'So, Sam Chambers is a friend of yours?' Emily asked bluntly, impatient to steer the conversation towards the missing boy.

Jamal nodded. 'Sam's my best friend. We were sharing a tent.'

Harry looked close to tears. 'I keep forgetting it's happened, then, whoosh, it all comes back.' He paused and gulped. 'Sam's a great guy. He's a brilliant footballer, you know. Arsenal have offered him a place on their youth squad . . .'

Scott felt a pang of envy. Being scouted to try out for Chelsea was his number one dream. Then he felt ashamed of himself. How could he be *jealous* of someone who was missing – a boy who might be lying somewhere injured, or being held prisoner, or even dead? 'I'm sure Sam will be OK,' he said kindly.

'Yeah, we'll help find him,' Jack added. 'We're good at mysteries. We've solved loads of them.'

'Do you have any idea what happened?' Emily asked.

Harry shook his head. 'We're not really meant to talk about it.'

Emily suddenly noticed that Jamal was staring at Jack as if he'd seen a ghost. 'That . . . is . . . so . . . freaky!' he stammered.

'Don't worry,' Scott joked. 'My brother always looks like that.'

'No, *that*!'

Everyone followed Jamal's gaze. Boz was peeping out over the collar of Jack's t-shirt, sniffing hopefully for more cheese.

'Sam has a pet mouse *exactly* like that!' Jamal murmured.

Jack grinned. 'I know. This is it.' He recounted the story of how he'd found the mouse at Bosgoose Cottage. 'The police have asked me to look after him until Sam gets back,' he added importantly.

'*Him?*' Jamal said, still staring as if bewitched by the gleaming pink eyes. 'Sorry mate, but that's a girl mouse. She's called Pasca.'

Jack stroked the soft white fur. *What sort of a name was Pasca?* And did he really want a *girl* mouse running around under his t-shirt? No, he was sure the mouse was much happier being a boy called Boz.

The ice creams arrived and there was silence – apart from a few slurps – as they all tucked in. Emily ate slowly. Somehow they had to get Harry and Jamal to spill what they knew about Sam's disappearance – if anything – before they finished their desserts and left. It was time to shake things up a bit.

'Of course, we know about all about Sam's connection with Medania,' she said casually.

Harry flushed even redder under his sunburn. Jamal's eyes flickered around the café as if worried someone might be listening from behind the display of fruit bowls hand-crafted by local potters. But the café was empty apart from Dotty chopping tomatoes behind the counter.

'How did you find out?' Jamal asked.

Scott, Emily and Jack exchanged excited glances. *How did you find out?* definitely meant they were on the right track!

Ten

Not Much to Go On

Emily's surprise tactic did the trick. Believing that the friends already knew half the story, Harry and Jamal decided it was safe to trust them with the rest of it. Scott, Jack and Emily listened in astonishment as the boys revealed that Sam Chambers was really Prince Sebastian Louis de Fiorello-Monteblanco, heir to the throne of Medania.

'If I had a fancy-schmancy name like that, I'd want

to change it, too!' Jack joked.

'It's supposed to be top secret for security reasons,' Jamal explained. 'He's been posing as Sam Chambers, ordinary son of an ordinary London doctor, ever since he came to Braithwaite School three years ago. But we've all known his true identity for ages!'

'So, d'you think he could have been kidnapped?' Scott asked. 'If he's royalty his family must have loads of money to pay a ransom.'

Jamal licked his spoon and nodded. 'Definitely.'

Emily shot him a searching look. 'Why are you so sure?'

Jamal shrugged. 'I saw these suspicious-looking guys lurking around . . .'

Suspicious-looking guys? Emily thought she'd died and gone to heaven! The pieces were all falling perfectly into place. The Medanian Mafia had kidnapped Prince Sebastian and were demanding a king's ransom for his release. Anya must have been discussing the arrangements for flying to Medania for the handover when Scott overheard her in the gorse bush!

Emily grabbed her phone from her bag and scrolled to a photograph she'd taken of Rudi, Anya and Nico when they were talking to Old Bob in the harbour. 'I think you'll find *these* are your suspicious characters!' she proclaimed, thrusting the phone under Harry and Jamal's noses.

Jamal glanced at the small screen. 'Yeah, they could be . . . I'm not sure . . .'

Harry shook his head. 'I wouldn't know. Jamal's the only one who saw them.' But he took the phone anyway and inspected the photograph. He looked up. 'No, it can't be this lot. We've seen these guys before.' He turned to Emily, Scott and Jack. 'They're like Medanian royal bodyguards or something. They come and check out the security arrangements for Sam at school every year. That's what made us suspect he had a secret identity in the first place. You don't get your own personal security team if your dad's a knee surgeon at North London Hospital! Don't you remember them, Jamal?'

Jamal looked again. 'Oh, yeah, you're right.'

Emily could hardly believe her ears. She'd been so sure the Medanians had abducted the missing boy she'd almost started writing CASE CLOSED in her notebook. 'So what are they doing sneaking around the school camp and diving into gorse bushes to avoid the police?' she spluttered. *And messing up my investigation*, she thought.

But Scott had already figured it out. 'If they work for the Medanian royal family, they've obviously come to try to find out what has happened to Prince Sebastian. The Carrickstowe police must have told them to keep out of it and let them get on with their investigation. I bet they're not licensed to be carrying guns here, either.'

Jack grinned. 'You mean they're in the same boat

as us – trying to investigate while keeping under D. I. Hassan's radar?'

Emily sighed. Scott was right, of course. She took out her ruler and neatly crossed out the entire *Suspects* section of Operation Missing Boy. The seven pages of details she'd painstakingly recorded about the Medanian Mafia were now totally useless. 'Back to Square One,' she complained.

'What about Jamal's dodgy-looking dudes?' Jack offered.

Emily instantly brightened up. She turned to Jamal, her pen poised over a fresh page of her notebook. 'OK, I need a precise date, time and location for each sighting . . . and full descriptions of each suspect . . .'

'Yes, she *is* always like this,' Jack said, before Harry and Jamal could ask.

Jamal's description of the men was vague, to say the least. One was tallish, one was sort of medium height, one could have been Asian, but he wasn't sure . . . Emily tutted as she took notes. Jamal would never cut it as a secret agent with such sub-standard observation skills. But he did a little better on times and locations. 'First time was up at those woods on Monday evening . . .'

'Bosgoose Wood?' Scott prompted.

Jamal rubbed his hands over his close-cropped hair. 'Yeah. We were doing some orienteering games. They drove up the track and just loitered there for a bit . . .'

'Near the stile?' Jack asked.

Jamal nodded. 'Yeah, that's right.'

'Details of the car?' Emily demanded. 'Make, year, registration number?'

Jamal tugged at his earlobes and looked sheepishly into his dish as if the pool of melted strawberry ice cream might jog his memory. 'Er, it was sort of silver. Or maybe grey.'

Emily resisted the temptation to scream.

'What about the second time?' Scott asked.

'That was on Tuesday. We were all at that hire shop next door to here – the Castle Key Cabin – getting kitted out with wetsuits for a jet-ski lesson.'

'It was in the morning, about nine,' Harry added, predicting Emily's next question.

Jamal chewed at the ragged edge of his thumbnail. 'That's right. I saw the same silver-grey car parked down the road.'

'Show me where!' With a screech of chair legs on the floor, Emily was up and heading for the door.

Powerless to resist – even though he was three times her size – Jamal followed Emily out of the café and pointed to a spot further along the seafront just outside the fish market. 'The car was there. Same three guys. They watched us for ages.'

Harry joined them, having stopped at the counter to pay. He checked his watch and made a face. 'Come on,' he told Jamal. 'We'd better get back to camp before The Rodmanator reports *us* missing too.'

'It's not much to go on,' Emily grumbled. 'Three men who might be tall or short . . .'

'. . . or Asian or not Asian,' Scott added. 'And a car that *might* be silver.'

'Or possibly grey,' Jack laughed. 'Do you think Jamal needs his eyes testing?'

The friends were conducting a fingertip search of the area outside the fish market where Jamal had sighted the suspicious car. But even Drift's super-sensitive nose was unable to sniff out anything more than a few scraps of raw fish. Either the men hadn't been considerate enough to drop any helpful clues or – since Jamal had given the same information to the police – PCs Patel and Kennedy had already bagged up the evidence and taken it away for analysis.

They gave up and set about questioning the fishermen in the harbour and the people working in the fish market. But nobody recalled seeing a silvery grey or greyish-silver car parked outside the market at nine o'clock on Tuesday morning.

'I'm sure we'd have noticed,' a plump lady remarked, looking up from gutting a mackerel. She looked like a kindly dinner lady in her white catering hat and apron, apart from the red-brown blood dribbling from her knife over her blue plastic gloves. 'That's where Terry Pender parks his van to pick up the day's fish for the

Grand Vista Hotel. He goes ape if someone takes his space.'

Emily jotted the name down in her notebook. Of course, she should have remembered about the Grand Vista van. She kept records of all the regular delivery times on the island – you never knew when they might come in useful. She would call Terry at the hotel right now and ask if he'd seen the car. Progress at last!

But the fish lady suddenly remembered something. 'Although Terry was late on Tuesday,' she said as she decapitated a sardine and threw the head into a bin. 'He didn't get here till gone ten . . . engine trouble or something.'

Emily snapped her notebook shut. Jamal's mystery men and their invisible car were proving as slippery as the fish guts spilling from the stainless steel workbenches.

All out of ideas, the friends wandered across the road and sat down on the harbour wall. Scott watched a group of tourists taking photographs of the colourful fishing boats in the harbour. If only someone had been taking photos outside the fish market on Tuesday morning, they might have captured the three men and their car. But how likely was that? Of course, a CCTV camera would be even better. Scott glanced back at the fish market. No camera. It was hardly surprising; he didn't imagine that raw mackerel was top of most burglars' wish-lists.

Scott scanned the row of shops along the seafront.

The only CCTV camera was mounted high on the wall of the Castle Key Cabin, watching over the expensive surfboards and bikes for hire on the racks outside. But that camera was no use. It pointed straight ahead, only taking in a small stretch of the seafront directly in front of the shop – he knew that for a fact, having seen some of the footage during Operation Skeleton. The skeleton had been caught on film just where that Fruity Fresh Juice van was parking now.

Scott screwed up his eyes, dazzled by the sunlight bouncing off the windscreen of the Fruity Fresh Juice van, the dark glass as shiny as a mirror.

Suddenly Scott had a brilliant idea. He leaped down from the wall and sprinted to the Castle Key Cabin.

Eleven

Gathering Evidence

Scott searched among the goods displayed outside the Castle Key Cabin, grabbed a deckchair, a child's red plastic bucket and a picnic basket and piled them into a rickety tower. Then he climbed to the top and looked across the seafront road at the van.

Reflected in the dark windscreen he could see deep blue sky, cotton wool clouds and a starburst of sunlight. He stood on tiptoes. Now his eyes were almost level

with the CCTV camera on the wall behind him and –
yes! – he could see the reflection of the buildings along
the seafront in the van's windscreen. Scott squinted into
the sun, but from this distance, and with the buildings
warped into tall, wavering towers by the curve of the
glass, he couldn't make out whether the fish market was
part of the reflection.

He looked down from his precarious perch to see
Emily, Jack and Drift staring up at him. 'Jack, go and
stand on the spot where Jamal said he saw the car,' he
ordered. 'And when you get there, start waving.'

Jack was about to suggest that if Scott wanted to
hang around outside fish markets waving like a total
wally he could do it himself, but then he had second
thoughts. Scott was balancing on a stack of assorted
beach equipment, staring out to sea with a manic look
on his face. Unless it was meant to be some kind of
performance art, it seemed his brother had finally
gone ga-ga. Jack shrugged and shuffled off along the
seafront.

Meanwhile, Scott kept his eyes fixed on the van.
After a few moments Jack's reflection appeared in
the windscreen, stretched and wobbly, but easily
recognizable from the red t-shirt, khaki shorts and blond
hair. The reflection walked along and then stopped and
held up a hand to wave. 'Success!' Scott cheered.

'Success?' Emily asked, looking up at Scott. 'Er, what
exactly are we successful *at*?'

'Gathering evidence!' Scott laughed, pulling Emily up onto the shaky tower.

Emily teetered on the edge of the picnic basket, not helped by Drift, who – thinking this was a new game – was trying to clamber aboard, too. Clinging to Scott's arm she followed his pointing finger, but all she saw was a man in Fruity Fresh Juice overalls get into his van and drive away.

'Agggh!' Scott yelled. 'He's going! My *mirror*!'

Emily was seriously beginning to wonder whether Scott needed medical attention when the picnic basket slipped off the bucket and the bucket buckled and the deckchair folded and the whole construction toppled over like a giant game of Jenga.

Emily crawled out from under the wreckage and extracted herself from the folded deckchair. Hearing a muffled yelp, she looked around for Drift. He was nowhere to be seen. She jumped as the picnic basket began to shuffle towards her. Then she laughed as she realized Drift was stuck underneath it, wearing it like a giant turtle shell. She freed Drift from the basket and looked round for Scott, waiting for an explanation. She hoped it was going to be a good one.

But Scott just sat up and pulled the bucket off his foot. 'Quick, give me your notebook and a pen!' he said.

Scott began covering pages in complicated diagrams and muttering to himself about angles, convex curves and reflections like a mad scientist. 'Ta da!' he cried at last, holding the notebook up to Emily. 'If a car is parked outside the fish market on the exact spot where Jack is now standing, the camera *here* can see it reflected in the windscreen of a vehicle parked over *there*.' He pointed across the road at the empty space where the Fruity Fresh Juice van had been. 'It'd be distorted by the curved glass, but we should be able to see the registration number as a mirror image on the CCTV film . . . and maybe the men, too.'

Emily stared at the diagram and grinned. At last Scott's antics were making sense. 'That's genius!'

But suddenly Scott sighed. 'Of course, it only works if there was a vehicle with a large windscreen parked exactly where that van was last Tuesday morning at nine.'

Now it was Emily's turn to go into hyperdrive. She snatched her notebook out of Scott's hands and flicked through it. 'Tuesday, let's see . . .' She ran her finger down a neatly written chart. 'I thought so! The Roshendra Farm lorry always delivers the ice cream for Dotty's café on Tuesday morning between eight-thirty and nine – and it parks right there.'

'Yes!' Scott shouted.

Emily looked up at the CCTV camera hardly able to contain her excitement. 'All we need to do now is get a look at that footage . . .'

Jack, meanwhile, was feeling decidedly *un*excited. He'd been standing outside the fish market waving like a deranged cheerleader for *centuries* now. His arms were dropping off. The pong of fish was getting up his nose. And people were giving him some very funny looks. 'It's *Jack do this, Jack do that*!' he grumbled. 'Why do I have to do all the work around here?'

From his perch on Jack's shoulder, Boz looked up with a sympathetic gleam in his pink eyes.

'You're right, mate. I shouldn't put up with it,' Jack said. 'Oy!' he yelled at the top of his voice. 'Can I stop doing this now?'

Scott heard the distant shout, glanced along the seafront and saw a figure in a red t-shirt jumping up and down outside the fish market. 'Oh, yeah, I forgot we'd left Jack there!'

Emily giggled. 'Let's go and tell him he can move before he's arrested for causing a public disturbance.'

Scott took another look at Jack. 'No hurry!' he said with a grin. 'And anyway,' he added, holding up the broken bucket, 'we'd better go in and pay for this first.'

It was Jack who came up with the plan for getting to see the footage from the CCTV camera. 'We could ask Theo Jarvis to help,' he suggested – after Scott and Emily had explained the Great Reflection Theory to him (*and* after Emily had forced Scott to apologize to Jack for leaving him stranded outside the fish market, and *then* forced Jack to accept the apology and agree to talk to his brother again).

Scott and Emily thought it was a great idea. Theo Jarvis was a friendly young surfing fanatic they'd met during Operation Compass. He'd now set up his own surf school and hire shop in Carrickstowe, but until recently he'd worked as an assistant at the Castle Key Cabin, owned by a lady called Mrs Phillips.

'Jack's right,' Emily said. 'I'm sure Theo could blag some excuse to go back into Mrs Phillips' office at the cabin and get a quick look at the CCTV images.'

Early next morning the friends cycled over the causeway to the mainland. They found Theo outside his new shop, The Surfing Pirate, at the end of Carrickstowe's bustling marina.

Theo – dressed in his usual stripy t-shirt, baggy shorts and flip-flops – was waxing a surfboard while entertaining a crowd of tourists with an unlikely yarn. 'Oh, yeah,' he drawled, 'surfing was first invented by pirates right here in Cornwall . . .' When he saw the friends he greeted them with high-fives all round. A few minutes later he took a break and joined them at a picnic table just outside the shop on the quayside. 'What can I do for you?' he asked, handing out cold bottles of Coke.

Scott explained their mission.

'Sure, I can help.' Theo raked his shaggy hair – bleached bone-white by sun and sea salt – out of his eyes. 'I owe you guys big-time. If you hadn't found the Pendragon smugglers' hoard I would never have got my share of the proceeds to invest in this place.'

'So can you get access to the CCTV footage at the Castle Key Cabin from nine on Tuesday morning?' Emily pressed. 'And make us a copy?'

'You'd better send a copy to the police as well,' Scott added. 'They probably won't have noticed the reflections.'

Emily nodded. She wanted to be the first to crack the case, of course, but the most important thing was to find the boy as soon as possible. If the kidnappers' car was visible on that CCTV camera they had to share the information with the police.

'Just don't tell them it was our idea,' Jack chipped in. 'We're supposed to be keeping our noses out, remember?'

Theo grinned and put his feet up on the table. 'No sweat. In fact, I was going to ask Mrs P if I could check out the camera system she's got at the cabin – see whether I want to install the same type here. I'll go this afternoon and take a look at those images for you while I'm there.' He glanced at his watch. 'Anyone fancy a surfing lesson? Looks like my ten o'clock is a no-show.'

After the awesomely exciting surf session and an enormous lunch of fish and chips on the pier, Jack was all for going to the fair. Scott, meanwhile, voted for a snooze on the beach, whereas Drift fancied checking out some rock pools.

But Emily had other ideas. 'While we're waiting for Theo to report back we can follow up on Jamal's other sighting of the suspicious men. If they drove up the track to Bosgoose Wood on Monday evening there'll be tyre tracks. Remember how muddy it was when we were cycling home?'

They eventually reached a compromise: half an hour chilling on the beach (with optional side trip to the rock pools) and two rides on the dodgems and a go on the helter-skelter before cycling back to Bosgoose Wood.

The friends searched the track to the stile. They soon found their own footprints and pawprints and the tracks left by their bikes on Monday afternoon. But there were no recent car tyre tracks in the mud.

Jack and Scott threw themselves down on a bank of heather. The sun was beating down and their water bottles were empty.

'If we'd stayed at the fair we could be eating ice creams right now,' Jack sighed. 'But oh, no, *someone* forced us to cycle hundreds of miles to look at non-existent tyre tracks.'

For once Scott was with Jack. 'Yeah, if we'd stayed on the beach we could be swimming in lovely cooool water . . .'

Drift flopped down next to the boys. He didn't say anything, of course, but he wished he was still splashing in the rock pools.

Emily stuck her tongue out at the three of them. She was just as fed up as they were. Jamal's suspicious men and their phantom car had given them the slip yet again. Now their hopes were pinned on the CCTV footage.

All they could do was wait for a call from Theo.

Twelve

Emily Takes a Short Cut

It was late in the evening and Scott was sitting on his bed running through some classic guitar riffs when his mobile phone rang. It was Theo Jarvis. The conversation started so well. Theo had called in at the Castle Key Cabin, wangled some time in Mrs Phillips' office alone and found the CCTV records from Tuesday morning.

Scott could hardly bear the suspense. 'Was the

lorry there?' he asked, trying to fast-forward Theo's laid-back account. '*Could you see the reflection?*'

'Yeah! The lorry was there. You could see the fish market in the windscreen, just like you figured.'

This is it! Scott made a thumbs-up sign at Jack, who was lying on the floor teaching Boz to drive a little toy car he'd found in the ancient toy box in the corner of their room.

'But there was no car there, dude,' Theo said. 'No dodgy guys hanging around. Zilch!'

Scott's thumbs-up slowly wilted to a thumbs-down. 'Are you sure you got the right time?'

'Yeah, it was when those school kids were there hiring their wetsuits. The camera's caught them milling around outside the shop. Your witness must have been seeing things!'

Scott hung up and threw himself back on his bed with a force that made the windows in the little attic bedroom rattle. Then he phoned Emily.

Sitting in her room at The Lighthouse, Emily frowned at her notebook as she listened to Scott's disappointing news. She drew a circle round the heading *OPERATION MISSING BOY.* There was a pattern forming here. None of the information Jamal had given them had panned out. *Maybe I should rename this case Operation Missing Clues,* she thought. Was Jamal just chronically confused, or had he been lying all along? 'But why?' she asked Drift, who was curled up on her bed. 'Why would you lie when your best friend's life could be at stake?'

Drift snuffled in his sleep.

Emily closed the *Teach Yourself Medanian* book she'd been studying. She scanned the shelf, took down a book entitled *Lie Detection: Theory and Methods* and began to read.

—

Emily peered at the time on her alarm clock. It was four fifteen in the morning and a quarter of an hour to go until first light. Even the seagulls were still asleep. She'd trained herself to wake at the slightest noise – a special agent had to be prepared for ambush at any time – and she could tell that Drift had heard something, too. His ears were standing to attention.

Emily opened her bedroom door a crack. Faint sounds were coming from six floors below. Footsteps padding, doors creaking, the zipping of a bag. It seemed that the Medanians – who were still staying at The Lighthouse pretending to be German holidaymakers – were up and about. Emily hesitated. Nico, Rudi and Anya were no longer suspects, but they *were* looking for the missing boy. And now they were heading out on a pre-dawn mission. Had they received some kind of tip-off about the whereabouts of Sam Chambers, a.k.a. Prince Sebastian?

'Come on, Drift,' Emily whispered. 'Let's find out!' She bundled her hair up into an elastic band, pulled black tracksuit bottoms and a sweatshirt on over her pyjamas and slung her bag over her shoulder.

Carrying Drift so that the clicking of his claws wouldn't give them away, she tiptoed down the spiral staircase as far as the second-floor landing, stopping only to chalk a note on the kitchen blackboard to say she had taken Drift out for an early-morning walk. She waited until she heard the front door open and close behind the Medanians, then flew down the rest of the stairs and peered through the window. Three shadowy figures were already melting into the grainy darkness.

Emily opened the door and hesitated for a moment, one hand flat against the smooth curved wall of The Lighthouse, feeling the cold seep into her palm. Then, with a whispered command to Drift to stay close, she slipped outside just as the palest glimmer of pink began to show in the eastern sky.

The Medanians moved quickly but Emily and Drift knew the terrain of the promontory so well that they were able to keep up, picking their way sure-footedly along the rocky path made slick by sea spray. Anya, Rudi and Nico jogged past the parking area and entered the maze of lanes and alleyways of Castle Key village. Emily and Drift followed, darting between parked cars, telephone boxes and garden walls. At the corner of Honeysuckle Lane, the Medanians stopped. Emily crouched behind a wheely bin and peeped out. The three figures – one huge, one tall and thin and one small and slim, all dressed in black and hunchbacked by their backpacks – were consulting a map in the orange glow of a streetlight.

Emily strained to hear their murmurs over the pounding of her heartbeat in her ears. They were speaking in Medanian, of course, but her studies paid off. She recognized a few of the phrases that drifted back to her on the still night air – 'meeting place', and 'thirty minutes' and then, best of all, *jebrinka karospo*.

Emily could hardly breathe for excitement. She hadn't bothered with learning the usual boring stuff in *Teach Yourself Medanian*, like *What is the soup of the day?* and *Do you sell postage stamps here?* She'd focused on phrases that might actually be useful to understand, phrases like *We have made contact with the kidnappers*, *Our snipers are in place* and *What time is the secret rendezvous?*

Which is how she knew that *jebrinka karospo* meant *ransom demand*.

Emily had to stop herself doing a victory jig. Rudi, Anya and Nico were going to rendezvous with someone in thirty minutes and it had something to do with a ransom demand! Was a messenger going to deliver a ransom note? Or could this even be the exchange itself? Perhaps those backpacks were stuffed with money that the Medanians were going to hand over to the kidnappers in return for the safe release of Prince Sebastian. Either way, Emily planned to be there.

But now Anya, Rudi and Nico were off again, silent and swift! Their training as royal bodyguards had clearly included an extreme fitness regime as well as stealth-mode operations. By the time they reached Castle Road and began racing up the steep hill Emily wasn't sure how much longer she could keep up with them. She was a good runner herself, but she was gasping for breath and falling behind. She couldn't bear to lose them now when they were so close . . .

Emily looked up the road to the ruins of the castle looming on the cliff, dark and foreboding against the charcoal and pink sky. Of course! This road wasn't called Castle Road for nothing. It didn't lead anywhere else. The castle had to be the meeting place.

'Come on, Drift,' Emily whispered. 'We'll take the short cut across the fields.' She hopped over a gate set into the hedge and trotted along the footpath at a steady pace, dew from the grass soaking into the bottoms of her track-pants. Drift bounded along enjoying the unexpected bonus of a lovely long walk while the enticing scents of night creatures were still fresh on the ground. Here and there trills floated up into the damp air as small birds began to tune up for the dawn chorus.

Emily was feeling very pleased with herself. She'd almost reached the stile on the other side of the field already. This path took ten minutes off the route by road. In fact, she even had a few seconds to spare to send a Situation Report text to the boys. She sat down on a fallen branch, took her phone from her bag and began typing. Drift sat at her feet, his tongue lolling.

Following MM. Meeting at cast—

Emily was about to press the 'l' and the 'e' keys when she sensed a movement behind her. She felt hot breath on the back of her neck and sprang off the log in blind terror, tripping over Drift and landing face down in the wet grass. She flipped over and pushed up onto her elbows, ready to fight for her life with every kick-boxing move she knew.

Thirteen

On the Trail

There was nobody there.

But in the deep shadow under the hedgerow, all around the branch where Emily had been sitting, a collection of huge hummocks was shifting and snorting. Now they were lumbering to their feet, gathering round her and nudging her with soft, slobbery muzzles.

Cows! Emily sat up and almost cried with relief. 'You really gave me a fright there, girls!' She reached out and patted a warm coarse-haired flank. Then she placed a hand on her chest and felt her heart still flapping around in her ribcage like a trapped sparrow. She looked down at Drift. 'Not a word of this to Scott and Jack, OK?'

Suddenly Emily remembered her phone . . . she'd dropped it when the cows startled her. She felt around in the damp grass until her fingers brushed against a cold hard corner. 'Yes!' she cried, and then 'Yuk!' as she felt the warm squelch of the fresh cowpat the phone had landed in. She quickly wiped the gloop off on the grass. Her half-finished message to Jack and Scott had disappeared from the screen, but there was no time to write it again. The Medanians would be at the castle any second. *I'll probably have solved the case by the time the boys wake up, anyway!* she thought, stuffing her phone in her bag. She called to Drift and ran to the stile.

Within moments, Emily was hiding in a holly bush at the edge of the castle ruins. She scanned the scene. The car park, the ruined towers and the museum building were all dark and silent. *I must have got here first.* Keeping low, and with Drift at her heels, she scooted across the grassed-over moat to the nearest tower, crept through a hole in the wall and climbed a crumbling stone staircase to a ramshackle wooden platform encrusted with bird droppings. The arrow slits in the thick stone wall of the tower provided a seagull's-eye view of the entire castle and its surrounds.

Emily watched through her binoculars for the

Medanians and the kidnappers to arrive. Then she tried her night-vision goggles, even though the sky was brightening as the red disc of the sun began to appear above the horizon. She checked her watch. She checked it again. It was almost forty minutes since the Medanians had said the meeting was in thirty. Gradually the terrible truth dawned on her. The rendezvous wasn't at the castle after all!

As she trailed back down the stairs Emily felt exhausted and hollow. But most of all, she felt furious with herself. Taking the short cut through the fields and losing sight of her targets had been an unforgivable tactical error. She walked out on to the cliff top, taking in the vast emptiness: the endless black rolling sea to the south, the lights of Castle Key village twinkling to the west, the miles of heathland to the north and east.

The Medanians could be anywhere by now.

She was about to head home when she noticed Drift snuffling in a tussock of grass. Then with a soft yip he sped away, nose to the ground and tail in the air. Emily opened her mouth to call him back; this was no time for chasing rabbits. But then she caught sight of something glinting in the grass. She stooped and picked up a small silver coin.

Rabbits didn't carry coins.

Especially not *Medanian* coins.

Drift had picked up their trail.

Meanwhile, in the attic bedroom at Stone Cottage, Jack was lying awake, thinking up new tricks to teach Boz. He was designing a miniature BMX bike in his head when he heard Scott's phone buzz on the bedside table on the other side of the room. It sounded like an incoming text message. He looked at the clock. Who was sending texts at four-thirty in the morning? It was probably just spam, but what if Dad was having some kind of archaeological emergency in Cambodia? Jack couldn't ignore it. He tiptoed across the room and checked the message.

It was from Emily: *Following MM. Meeting at cast*

Jack shook Scott's shoulder.

'Uggh!' Scott moaned.

'Message from Emily!' Jack's shoulder-shaking became more urgent.

'If it's summoning us to another of her crack-of-dawn meetings, tell her to get lost!' Scott snapped, sticking his head under his pillow.

'Following MM?' Jack said, thinking aloud. 'I guess that means the Medanian Mafia. But what's *meeting at cast*?'

'Meeting at cast?' Scott's voice was muffled by the pillow. 'That doesn't even make sense.'

'It might be a code,' Jack suggested.

'Yeah,' Scott sighed. 'It's Emily. That figures.'

Jack stared at the screen until his eyes went fuzzy. *Meeting at cast* didn't look like code. But how could the meeting be *at cast*? *Cast* wasn't a place. Maybe she meant somewhere else but had spelled it wrong? He tried to think of places that sounded like *cast*. Carrickstowe? Quarry? They were too different. *Castle* . . . yes, that could be it! But Emily never made spelling mistakes! Jack was about to give up and go back to bed when another thought struck him. *Cast* was the first four letters of *castle.* What if something – or *someone* – had stopped Emily finishing the message . . .

All at once, Jack was throwing on his clothes and dive-bombing Scott's bed. 'Em's at the castle and she's in trouble!' he cried as Boomerang shot out from under him with an indignant squawk. 'We've got to go and help her!'

Scott shoved Jack off and burrowed his head further under the pillow.

'Suit yourself! Me and Boz will go on our own!' Jack scooped the sleeping mouse from his nest of shredded tissue and popped him in his shorts pocket. 'We don't need you.'

Scott groaned. If Emily was in trouble the last thing she needed was Jack charging in with one of his daredevil rescue stunts.

He rolled out of bed and felt around for his trainers.

—

Back on the cliff top Drift and Emily were still on the trail of the Medanians. They'd run along the coast path for some time and had cut inland onto the remote headland above Pirate Cove. Emily was beginning to wonder whether Drift really was chasing a rabbit. There was nothing up here but a few sheep and wild ponies.

Emily stopped under cover of a thicket of gorse and bramble to catch her breath. The seagulls were awake now and crying so loudly that she didn't hear the whirring noise until it was almost directly overhead. She looked up through the branches to see an unmarked black helicopter. *Of course, that's how the kidnappers are getting here,* she thought. *No wonder they need to meet in a remote location!* But where were Anya, Rudi and Nico?

That's when she felt breath on her neck.

This time it wasn't a cow.

Emily heard Drift growl but, before she could call him, a hand was clamped over her mouth. Then everything went black.

Fourteen

Hostage!

Scott and Jack jumped on their bikes and bombed down Church Lane and along the deserted high street as if pursued by a pack of wild hyenas. The streetlights were still on but the sky had lightened to the pale pink shade of the inside of Boz's ears. The boys stood up on their pedals and pounded their way up Castle Road, the chill salty air burning in their lungs.

Emily jabbed both elbows into her attacker's sides and aimed a high-speed back-kick at what her kick-boxing coach called the 'trouser area'. But whoever had grabbed her from behind was obviously trained in martial arts too. They caught Emily by the ankle, swung her into the air and flipped her over. It could have been an ice-dancing lift except that it ended with Emily crash-landing on her back – winded, disoriented and pinned down by a knee on her chest and hands gripping her wrists.

She struggled but it was no good. She was held fast. Emily opened her eyes but she couldn't see because a hood had been pulled over her head. She tried to gulp air into her lungs but the material was sucked into her mouth and nostrils with each breath. Hot molten panic surged through her veins. She fought it back, forcing herself to keep calm and breathe slowly while she tried to make sense of what was happening.

Around her three voices were speaking urgently in Medanian. Gradually Emily began to pick up fragments of the argument: *tie her up . . . in the helicopter . . . to London . . .*

Panic took hold again. Emily writhed and bucked against her captor's grasp. She didn't want to be taken to London in a helicopter! And where was Drift? Suddenly the cover was yanked away from her head.

She blinked in the light and tried to focus on the face looming above her own, so close she could smell the mint-fresh toothpaste.

It was Anya.

Rudi and Nico were standing behind her on either side.

Now she could actually see her ambushers Emily suddenly felt a whole lot better. True, Anya still had her pinned to the ground and, true, Rudi and Nico were pointing guns at her, but the Medanians knew her from The Lighthouse. They'd played Scrabble together, for goodness' sake! *They'll soon realize I'm harmless and let me go.*

'What are you doing here?' Anya demanded in English.

I just have to act innocent, Emily thought, *and come up with a good reason to be wandering around on the headland at daybreak.* 'It's me, Emily, from The Lighthouse,' she said breezily. 'I was just out picking blackberries.' *Keep it simple,* she told herself, remembering the words of *Lie Detection: Theory and Methods*. Liars always over-complicate their story.

Anya eyed the blackberries growing on the bramble bushes all around them. They were small and red and wouldn't be ripe for another month. When she looked back at Emily her eyes were as cold and hard as flint.

'They're best picked early in the season for making,

er, chutney,' Emily added. She forced a smile. *Stay relaxed. Liars look nervous.*

At last Anya seemed to buy the blackberry story. She frowned for a moment then loosened her grip on Emily's wrists and stood up. Emily winced with pain as the blood began pumping back into her hands. Anya signalled to Rudi and Nico. The two men took a step back and lowered their guns.

Emily sat up and rubbed her sore wrists. 'Phew! For a minute there I thought you were going to tie me up and take me to London!'

As soon as the words had left her mouth Emily realized she'd blown it.

—

Scott and Jack searched every corner of every tower, walkway and dungeon, but Emily was not at the castle.

Scott headed back to the portcullis where he'd left his bike. 'If it turns out she's tucked up in bed at The Lighthouse you're for it!' he called back to Jack.

Jack trailed after Scott but he was sure Emily wasn't at home in bed. He'd called her mobile and sent her three texts. She always kept her phone under her pillow in case of vital nocturnal communications. She would have replied. Something was wrong.

Scott was on his bike pulling out onto Castle Road when something came hurtling out of the shadows towards him. He swerved and missed the speeding animal but hit a pothole and flew over the handlebars.

'Drift!' Jack shouted. 'Are you alright?'

'Don't worry about me,' Scott muttered, from under his front wheel. 'Just a few broken bones here.'

Jack hurried to Drift and hugged him. When he let go he saw rusty red streaks down the front of his t-shirt. With a cold, sick feeling in the pit of his stomach Jack lifted Drift's head. There was blood matted in the black and tan fur around his jaw. 'You idiot! You've run over Drift!' Jack yelled.

Scott crawled out from under his bike and ran to Drift's side. 'But the bike didn't touch him!' he said, elbowing Jack aside and examining Drift's face. 'I'm sure of it!' He turned to Jack. 'Look, he's just scratched his mouth. Like he's chewed on something spiky . . .'

Jack looked for himself and realized Scott was right. But he was still worried. Drift was panting as if he'd run a marathon. His ears were tucked flat against his head and his tail hung between his legs. 'You look terrible, Drifty. Where's Emily?'

Drift whimpered softly.

Jack was really scared now. He knew that Drift would never leave Emily's side unless it was a matter of life and death. He looked at Scott and could see that he knew it too.

Drift barked once, then ran off along the coast path back towards the headland. After a little way he turned, looked back at the boys and barked again before continuing along the path.

Filled with dread, Scott and Jack ran after him.

—

Nico grabbed hold of Emily from behind. She tried to bite the huge, hairy tattooed arm that had clamped itself across her chest, but he adjusted his grip and with his other hand he pulled her arm up behind her back. 'So, you just happen to speak Medanian, do you?' Nico demanded, twisting her arm as he leaned over to roar in her ear.

Emily flinched at the jolt of pain in her shoulder joint. 'No, of course not!'

'So how did you know we were talking about taking you to London in the helicopter?' Anya sneered. 'And don't try telling me they teach Medanian in English schools!'

'Admit it!' Rudi accompanied each word with a wave of his gun. 'You're working for the NMF, aren't you?'

'The NMF?' Emily gulped. 'I don't know what you're talking about.'

'Don't act the innocent with us!' Anya spat. 'The New Medania Faction. I knew I'd heard someone spying on us the other night at The Lighthouse!'

Rudi gave a bitter laugh. 'It's typical of those low-life traitors to recruit kids to do their dirty work!'

Emily shook her head. 'I've never even been to Medania. I'm just an ordinary girl from Castle Key!'

'Oh, yeah? So how do you explain this?' Emily looked round to see Rudi crouching down, looking at the scattered contents of her shoulder bag which she'd dropped in the struggle. For the first time in her life she wished she'd been carrying an *ordinary girl* handbag with lip gloss, hairbrush and Justin Bieber pencil case. Instead of . . .

'Night-vision goggles?' Rudi sneered. 'Fingerprint kit? Listening device?' He held up *Survival Guide for Secret Agents* and waved it in Emily's face. 'This comes in useful for blackberry picking, does it?'

Emily closed her eyes. There was no answer to that question. She'd always longed to be taken seriously as a secret agent. But right now she'd do anything to convince the Medanians she *wasn't* a spy. She knew her only chance was to come clean. 'Look, I'm not working for the NMF – whoever they are – but I do know you're working for the Medanian royal family and you're meeting Prince Sebastian's kidnappers here . . . Is that them up there?' she added, glancing up at the helicopter which was now coming in to land. It was so close she had to shout over the noise of the rotors. The downdraft was flattening the gorse and heather all around them.

Anya narrowed her eyes suspiciously. 'Don't play games with us!' she yelled. 'You know as well as I do that the NMF have kidnapped Sebastian. The king received their ransom note last night. They've taken him to London. There's where we're going now.'

The helicopter touched down and sat rocking on its runners. The pilot leaned out of the door, beckoning and shouting for the Medanians to hurry up.

'Bring the girl,' Anya commanded Rudi and Nico. 'She could be useful. If she's an NMF operative we can use her as a bargaining tool. We'll refuse to hand her back to them unless they give us Prince Sebastian, or at least agree to drop some of their demands. Now, move!'

'Excellent! A hostage!' Nico laughed, bundling Emily roughly towards the open doors of the helicopter. 'Let's see how much you're worth to your NMF spymasters, shall we?'

Emily stumbled along staring at the ground beneath her feet. She'd been in some tight corners before but she couldn't see how she was going to get out of this one. She might never see Castle Key again.

She just hoped that Drift had run to safety.

Fifteen

Storming In

Drift knew he had to keep running.

He was so tired even his tail was aching. His paws were sore and the scratches on his muzzle were stinging like crazy. He'd thought those humans were playing when they first jumped out on Emily. They'd seemed friendly enough at The Lighthouse, but then he'd smelled their aggression and Emily's fear . . . Drift had growled and snarled and tried to guard Emily, but the huge man had dragged him away and tied him up to a gorse bush. The branch wasn't thick but it was covered in thorns that tore at the soft flesh of his mouth and nose as he gnawed through it. But at last he was free. He'd slipped away before the man could tie him up again and he'd run to fetch help.

It had been a stroke of luck finding the boys at the castle! He'd thought he'd have to run all the way to Stone Cottage to fetch them. Drift looked back. Scott and Jack were puffing along the coastal path behind him. Why were humans so slow? They were almost back at the bramble patch now. He pricked up his ears and searched for Emily's voice but all other sounds were drowned out by a mechanical whirring. He flopped down in the dry bracken, too exhausted to go another step . . . he'd have to leave it to the boys now . . . they'd know what to do.

Scott and Jack dived behind the brambles, panting and gasping and holding their hands over their ears against the deafening roar of the helicopter. Jack crawled to the edge of the bushes and looked out. At first he couldn't see anyone, but then he spotted figures close to the helicopter. He recognized the mighty bulk of Nico leaning in through the open doors, manhandling the bundle in his arms to Rudi, who was reaching down from inside. The bundle was wriggling and kicking. Jack glimpsed arms and legs and long brown hair.

The bundle was Emily!

'We've got to save her!' Jack yelled, bursting out of the bushes.

Scott grabbed his arm. 'We can't just storm in! We need a plan.'

'Stuff plans!' Jack shouted. 'They've got Emily!'

Scott looked at the helicopter. Emily was almost in through the door. The rotor blades were accelerating to a blur ready for take-off. For once Jack was right! Storming in was the only option. He'd have to try to think of a plan on the way. '*Charge!*' Scott yelled, and together the boys hurtled towards the helicopter, heads down against the tornado force of the rotor blades.

Jack leaped onto Nico's back. Nico shrugged him off like an angry bull in a rodeo.

'Stop!' Scott screamed, tugging at Anya's jacket. 'What are you doing?'

Anya whipped round. 'She's spying for the NMF. We're taking her with us!'

Scott had no idea what Anya was talking about. 'She's not spying for anyone,' he shouted back. 'She's just a nosy kid!'

'Oh, yeah! A kid who speaks Medanian and carries night-vision goggles!' Nico scoffed.

'She just likes to play at detectives!' Scott knew Emily was going to kill him for those words if they ever got out of this, but it was a risk he was going to have to take.

'Whatever!' Nico yelled. 'She's coming with us.' He shoved Emily up to Rudi who grabbed her by the shoulders. The helicopter skids left the ground and Anya stepped onto the small metal ladder that hung down from the door.

Scott still didn't have a plan.

Nico held onto the doorframe ready to swing up after Anya. In one last desperate move, Jack dived at Nico's legs and clung on. Nico kicked him off as easily as shaking dog poo off his shoe. But then, just as it seemed it was all over, Nico shrieked and doubled over, swatting frantically at his trouser leg. He screamed again, a single word: *Chanko-o-o-o-o!*

Taken by surprise by Nico's screams, Rudi let go of Emily. She fell against Anya. Anya lost her balance and dropped backwards off the ladder into the bracken below. Emily landed on top of her.

Emily saw her chance and took it. She sprang away and ran for her life. She didn't stop until she was past the bramble bushes. Jack and Scott were right behind her.

Scott looked over his shoulder to see the helicopter rising into the sky, backlit by the huge red sun. Rudi and Nico were leaning out of the doorway pulling Anya inside. Her legs were dangling but she just made it aboard.

'What does *chanko* mean in Medanian?' Scott asked.

'I think it means *rat*!' Emily replied, laughing as Drift licked her nose. 'That must be what Nico was . . .'

Jack patted his pockets. 'Oh, no! Where's Boz?'

When Emily and Drift slipped back into The Lighthouse her parents were still in bed. It was almost midday when her mum knocked on the bedroom door, worried that Emily was ill. 'I've never known you sleep in so long,' she said. 'Or Drift, for that matter!'

'I'm fine. I just didn't sleep very well last night,' Emily told her. It was the truth, after all, just not quite the *whole* truth!

~

'Can you believe it?' Jack laughed, selecting a sandwich from the picnic lunch he'd brought along to the debriefing meeting at Bosgoose Cottage HQ. 'A great ogre like Nico being scared of a tiny little mouse! And calling Boz a rat, too!' He broke the corner off his cheese and pickle sandwich and offered it to Boz. To Jack's delight it turned out that his trusty friend hadn't hitched a ride to London inside Nico's trousers last night, but had dropped back into the bracken, where Jack had found him – along with Emily's bag – as the Medanians' helicopter disappeared into the crimson glow of the sunrise.

Scott grinned. 'Yeah, being scared of mice is nearly as pathetic as being phobic about, ooh, I don't know . . . *spiders*!'

'Uh-uh! Spiders are evil eight-legged mutants. Mice

are cool. If Boz hadn't given Nico the heebie-jeebies, Em would've been tied up and handed over to a gang of Medanian terrorists by now . . .'

'I can't help it if I'm such a convincing secret agent that they believed I was spying for an enemy organization,' Emily interrupted. 'Not *everyone* thinks that I "play at detectives".' She looked pointedly at Scott. She still hadn't quite forgiven him for those words.

Jack stroked Boz's ears. 'We make a great team.'

'Team!' Scott snorted. 'Boz jumped out of your pocket when you fell over! It was a solo effort.'

'No way! It was a carefully co-ordinated manoeuvre. I *staged* that "fall" so we could catch Nico off guard!'

Emily and Scott both laughed. 'Anyway,' Scott said, 'if anyone should take the credit for rescuing Emily, it's Drift!'

Drift pricked up his ears at the mention of his name. He was lying on his back toasting his fur in the sunshine, too tired even to chase rabbits. He wouldn't be able to pick up their scents anyway – the ointment that Emily had smeared all over the scratches on his muzzle was clogging up his nostrils with a disgusting *clean* smell. He stretched contentedly. Emily, Jack and Scott were safe. That was all that mattered.

Emily knelt and folded Drift in a hug. 'I still don't know how he got all the way to Stone Cottage to fetch you guys so quickly. He must have run like the wind.'

'We weren't *at* Stone Cottage,' Jack told her. 'We got

your text message and went to the castle.'

Emily looked up, puzzled. 'What message?'

'The one that said *Meeting at cast*. I used my mind-blowing powers of deduction and worked out you meant *castle*, of course.'

Emily stared at Jack. *Cast?* What was he talking about? 'I dropped my phone,' she explained, leaving out the minor detail of the cow-fright. She took out her phone and scanned the list of sent messages. There it was: *Following MM. Meeting at cast*— 'Oh, yeah,' she laughed. 'The SEND key must have got pressed when it hit the ground.'

Emily put her phone back in her bag and stood up. She kicked at a pile of rubble with her toe. 'Thanks for saving me,' she mumbled.

Jack cupped his hand behind his ear. 'Sorry, didn't quite catch that. Was that an official thank you from a top NMF agent?'

'I think it was!' Scott laughed.

Emily had known the boys long enough to be used to their teasing and couldn't help grinning as she wandered into the abandoned garden at the side of the cottage. Gnarled fruit trees and old raspberry canes were all draped in swathes of ivy and bindweed like a scene from Sleeping Beauty.

Jack and Scott followed her. 'Hey, there are still raspberries growing on here!' Jack cried. He picked a handful and stuffed them into his mouth. 'So who *are* these NMF people you're meant to be working for, anyway?' he asked.

'I did some research on the internet this morning. The NMF are the New Medania Faction,' Scott said, pacing around the raspberry canes as he spoke.

He just needs a whiteboard and a pointer, Jack thought, *and he'd make a perfect history teacher.*

'The NMF believe that the rightful heir to the throne of Medania isn't Prince Sebastian but some second cousin of his called Ferdinand. There was a big bust-up between the two sides of the royal family in the nineteenth century. The NMF has been fighting to get King Orlando to hand over the throne to Ferdinand for years.'

'And now they've kidnapped Sebastian?' The bright red raspberry juice trickling down Jack's chin made him look like a greedy vampire. 'I wonder how much they're asking for.'

'I don't think they're after money at all,' Scott explained. 'I bet they're refusing to hand Sebastian back until the king agrees to sign the throne over to this Ferdinand guy.'

'Well, they're in London now. Nothing more we can do!' Jack said, heading off to fetch a sandwich bag to collect some more raspberries for later. 'Anyone fancy going to the water park this afternoon?' he called over his shoulder.

Emily sat down on a tree stump and opened her

notebook. She'd written up the events of the night before but it looked so *untidy* with an empty page where the *Solution* section should be. She flicked back through her notes. There was still one loose end that needed to be tied up. 'Jamal,' she murmured, 'and his invisible clues . . .'

'I guess those suspicious guys he saw hanging around must have been this NMF gang,' Scott said, sprawling out in the long grass under an ancient pear tree.

Emily sighed. 'So why couldn't we see their car on the CCTV camera? Or the tyre tracks?'

Jack looked up from picking raspberries. 'So, what are you saying? Jamal was telling porky pies?'

'I'm sure of it,' Emily said. 'When he was telling us about seeing those men he kept touching his face and his hair. That's a classic sign of lying.'

Jack made a mental note to sit on his hands next time he was giving one of his world-famous late homework excuses. 'But *why* would Jamal say he saw the kidnappers if he didn't?'

Suddenly Scott sat upright. 'What if *he's* the one working with the NMF? He could have been scattering those false clues around to throw the police – and us – off the scent.'

Emily jumped to her feet. 'I think we need to ask Jamal a few more questions.'

'I guess that's a rain check on the water park then,' Jack muttered.

Sixteen

Ransom Note Received

Emily, Scott and Jack climbed the beech tree at the edge of Bosgoose Wood and looked out over the heath. The Braithwaite School camp was bustling with boys and teachers lugging equipment towards the jeeps.

'Uh-oh! How're we going to get past the Rodmanator?' Jack groaned. The discipline-with-a-capital-D teacher was keeping a close eye on Harry and Jamal as they dismantled a tent.

But Emily already had an idea. 'Jack, have you still got that bag of raspberries in your backpack?'

'You want a raspberry *now*?' Jack asked. 'Halfway up a tree?'

Emily shook her head and quickly explained her plan . . .

Moments later, the three friends were staggering into the school camp, Scott carrying Drift in his arms.

'Help!' Emily sobbed. 'My dog's hurt.' *Well, it's true,'* she thought. *Drift has hurt himself. I didn't say anything about when it happened.*

The schoolboys all crowded round looking at the scratches on Drift's face – which had been freshened up just a little with raspberry juice 'blood' matted into the fur.

Drift played his part to perfection, whimpering feebly.

'What's going on here?' Mr Rodman elbowed his way through the gaggle of boys, but his gruff manner softened as soon as he saw the wounded dog. 'Doesn't look too serious,' he told Emily. 'He's probably run through a gorse bush.'

While Mr Rodman hurried away to fetch the first aid kit, Scott beckoned to Harry and Jamal. 'Drift's fine,' he explained. 'We just wanted to talk to you.'

'Your mate is in London being held hostage by the NMF,' Jack chimed in.

'Yeah, we know,' Harry said. He looked so miserable,

136

even his blond quiff was drooping. 'D. I. Hassan came and told us this morning. The police were sent a copy of the ransom note.'

Emily turned to Jamal. 'We checked out your sightings of the suspicious men you saw hanging around. There was no one there.'

'I probably just got the times mixed up. I'm always doing that.' Jamal gave a goofy grin. '*Muddle* should be my middle name.'

'Tell me what the car looked like again,' Emily asked.

'Like I said, sort of silver . . .'

'Hatchback or saloon?'

'Saloon, I think. Yeah, it was quite big. Sorry, I'm hopeless at cars,' Jamal laughed.

Before Emily could ask another question, Mr Rodman was back. He gently dabbed Drift's muzzle with antiseptic ointment. Drift wrinkled his nose in disgust. Just when the smell of the last lot was wearing off, too!

'Right, you lot!' Mr Rodman's sergeant-major moustache bounced up and down as he hollered at the schoolboys. 'Show's over! Back to work!'

Scott, Jack and Emily left the tent and said goodbye to Harry.

Jamal was nowhere to be seen.

'Jamal probably just wanted to get away from Em staring into his eyes,' Jack said as they headed back towards the woods. 'I think she fancies him!'

Emily punched Jack's arm. 'I wasn't staring *into* his eyes. I was staring *at* them!'

'Oh, that's different then!' Scott laughed. 'Not!'

Emily stopped and faced the boys, her hands on her hips. 'It says in *Lie Detection: Theory and Methods*, that when people are telling lies they tend to look to the right. It's something to do with which bit of the brain they're using. Guess which way Jamal was looking!'

Jack wasn't sure about Emily's roving eyeball theory, but he was beginning to suspect she was right about Jamal. While poor Harry had seemed totally gutted by Sam-slash-Sebastian's disappearance, Jamal had been laughing and cracking jokes. *I like to clown around as much as anyone*, Jack thought, *but if one of my best mates had been kidnapped I'm sure I wouldn't be that chirpy.*

'Hey! Isn't that Jamal over there?' Scott asked.

Jack's thoughts were interrupted by Scott looking back and pointing at a stocky figure hurrying away from the camp towards the coast.

Emily grabbed her binoculars. 'Yes! He's making for the cliffs above Chicken Bay.'

Without a word the friends followed. They tore across the heath, skirted the camp and crouched behind a rocky mound near the cliff path. They peeped out and watched Jamal, who was standing close to the edge gazing out to sea.

'What's he doing?' Scott murmured. 'Meditating?'

Just when it seemed as though nothing would happen, Jamal took a small object from his pocket and held it up. There was a blinding flash as sunlight bounced off a reflective surface.

'It's a mirror!' Emily gasped. 'I think he's signalling . . .'

'Who to?' Jack asked. 'Passing seagulls?'

Scott looked out across the water. There was nothing out there. The police divers and the coastguard had all packed up and left now that the missing boy was known to be in London. But then Scott caught sight of a flash among the dark rocks of a small island about half a mile out in the middle of the bay. And then another. 'There's someone signalling back,' he breathed. 'It's Morse code!'

'Of course!' Emily rooted in her bag for her notebook and began jotting down the sequences of long and short flashes. 'Dot-dash-dot,' she mumbled. 'Dot-dash, then dash-dot and dot-dot-dot . . .'

Jack looked over her shoulder and read the letters as Emily deciphered Jamal's message. *R-a-n-s-o-m n-o-t-e r-e-c-e-i-v-e-d.*

There was a moment's pause, then the flashes started up on the island again: *I-s i-t s-a-f-e t-o m-o-v-e.*

N-o-t y-e-t, Jamal signalled back.

Jack's mouth dropped open. It seemed the kidnappers hadn't taken Sebastian to London at all – that was a false trail. They were holding him under their noses, right here in Castle Key.

And Jamal was working with them.

Seventeen

Walking on Water

'Did that just happen?' Scott asked, watching Jamal
hurry back towards the school camp. 'Or did I
imagine it?'

Emily looked at the message she'd transcribed in her
notebook. 'It happened all right. The kidnappers are on
Black Rock Island.'

Black Rock Island? The name fits, Scott thought.
The small island was dark and steep-sided and craggy.

141

'What's there?' he asked.

'Nothing but some caves and a couple of tiny beaches,' Emily said.

'What are we waiting for?' Jack asked. 'Sounds like we've got a rescue mission on our hands.'

Scott shook his head. 'Shouldn't we call D. I. Hassan and let the police handle it?'

Emily frowned. 'Jamal will just warn the kidnappers if he sees a load of police boats lining up to storm the island.'

'But he'll warn them if he sees *us* going there as well,' Scott pointed out. 'We'd get to Black Rock Island to find the kidnappers waiting to ambush us.'

'Not if Jamal doesn't see us.' Emily closed her notebook. 'I've got a plan. We take *Gemini* as far as Forgotten Cove, hide the boat there and climb over the rocks into Chicken Bay. We'll be tucked right under the cliffs so Jamal won't be able to see us from the top. Then we walk across to Black Rock Island.'

Scott and Jack looked at each other. *Walk* to the island? True, Emily had been a bit big-headed since the Medanians mistook her for a real spy – but surely she didn't think she could walk on water!

Emily laughed at their baffled expressions. 'There's a causeway. It's a sandbank just under the water. You can cross easily when the tide's out. I've just remembered something else, too,' she added. 'Mum said we were allowed to go camping on Black Rock Island. We can use that as our cover story for going there!' She rummaged in her bag for her *Discover Castle Key* guidebook, turned to the tide tables at the back and ran her finger down a column of numbers. 'Next low tide is at four o'clock.'

Scott checked his watch. 'That's only an hour and a half away. Can we make it?'

But Jack, Emily and Drift were already haring towards the woods. 'Of course we can,' Jack shouted over his shoulder. 'Last one to the bikes is a stinky snotbucket!'

—

Emily flew into The Lighthouse where her mum was in the guest lounge chatting to Mrs Loveday who'd dropped in for a gossip.

Emily skidded to a halt in the middle of the room. Drift cannonballed into her legs, nearly bowling her over. 'Camping!' she panted. 'Black Rock Island! We do want to go!'

'OK. When?' her mum asked.

Emily doubled over to catch her breath. 'Now!' she gasped.

'I'll call Old Bob and check that he's still night fishing out there.'

But Emily was already rocketing up the spiral staircase like a human tornado. 'Done it already!' she shouted from the sixth-floor landing. 'He is!'

'Young people today,' Mrs Loveday tutted. 'Always in such a hurry.'

Emily grabbed her backpack from her room – her survival kit was still packed from when she'd been planning the trip to Gulliver's Island – and ran back down the stairs, taking them three at a time.

By the time the boys came sprinting down the promontory Emily had already cast *Gemini* off from her moorings and started the outboard motor. Scott and Jack threw in their rucksacks and hopped aboard. Drift barked happily. He loved boat trips!

'Hardly had time to pack anything to eat!' Jack grumbled.

'Only the entire contents of Aunt Kate's fridge,' Scott laughed. 'Including half a tin of Boomerang's cat food!'

'There was no time to be *selective*,' Jack retorted. 'Anyway, you'll be begging to share my Whiskas meaty chunks after a few days of raw fish.'

At least we don't have to row *all the way there,* Scott thought as he cranked the motor up to the limit. Soon they had passed Pirate Cove, rounded the headland and were nosing into the tiny natural harbour of Forgotten Cove, hidden behind its curtain of rock. They tied *Gemini* up securely, shouldered their backpacks and squeezed through a porthole carved out of the rocky wall by the waves. They came out onto a fringe of rock-strewn beach at the base of the cliffs and made their way northwards, clambering over the boulders that blocked their way like climbing walls on a giant assault course. In places they had to pass Drift up and down between them. It was hot, tiring work but at last they came to the flatter, wider shoreline of Chicken Bay, where they were able to run unhindered. It was five o'clock already. There was no time to lose.

'Where's this causeway?' Jack puffed, as they drew level with Black Rock Island. He scanned the sparkling waves rolling in and out of the bay. Wave after wave. Nothing but waves.

'It's right here!' Emily pointed at the water lapping at their feet. At last Jack could see it. A strip of lighter blue was all that betrayed the sandbar under the surface.

Scott raised his binoculars. There was nothing moving on Black Rock Island apart from the gulls. 'Coast's clear!'

'Quick! The tide will be on its way in now. Let's cross while we still can,' Emily urged.

Scott felt his heart racing as they speed-waded along the submerged path through the knee-deep water. Emily's plan had worked fine so far, but out here on the causeway they were horribly exposed to view. He kept his eyes fixed on the island, expecting at any moment to see the kidnappers pop their heads up from behind the rocks, peer into their viewfinders and take aim. This must be how it felt to walk across a minefield, knowing that every step could be your last.

'If we see anything,' he told the others, 'we dive off the edge of the sandbar and swim. They won't be able to pick us off in the water.' He tried to sound surer of that last point than he felt.

You can always rely on Scott to look on the dark side! Jack thought. He'd been enjoying his walking-on-water experience until Scott had started going on about diving into the sea to avoid snipers. Jack wasn't the world's strongest swimmer. Not to mention the fact that he had Boz in his pocket. He was pretty sure that mice weren't big swimmers either, so he'd have to hold him up out of the waves somehow . . .

Luckily for Jack – and Boz – it didn't come to that. Fifteen minutes later they were safely on Black Rock Island, scrambling up onto the craggy rocks and then picking their way along a narrow steep-sided ravine that led inland. Stunted hawthorn trees clung to the high sides, their twisted branches reaching out to form a lacy ceiling that made the ravine into a cool dark tunnel. The friends crept along in single file, past even narrower gullies and crevasses that branched off to left and right, shooting nervous glances over their shoulders and jumping at the sound of every pebble skittering over the rocks. The kidnappers could be lurking anywhere in this maze.

But eventually the ravine came out on the other side of the island. Jack blinked as his eyes adjusted to the glare of sunlight after the deep shade. Gradually a small beach of fine white sand came into focus. There was a scattering of driftwood and seaweed and . . . something else . . . A trail of footprints tracked all the way along the empty beach to the far end, where a wall of rock rose up, riddled with holes like a giant honeycomb.

'They must be hiding in the caves!' Emily breathed.

'Strange,' Scott murmured. 'There's only *one* set of prints.'

Jack shrugged. 'Come on, let's follow them.'

The friends stole along the beach, watching for movement and listening for any sound above the shrieking of the gulls.

They reached the caves and peeped inside the first opening. Deep within, a faint light glowed for a second. Then it went out.

Jack's heart leaped into his throat.

In that fleeting flicker of light he'd glimpsed a pale, frightened face.

Eighteen

Stealth Mode

'Sam Chambers,' Jack whispered. 'I'm *sure* it was him!'

Scott pulled Jack away from the cave mouth. 'Careful! The kidnappers could be in there too.'

Emily leaned back against the rock and closed her eyes to think. How could they rescue Sam without being captured themselves? She opened them just in time to see Drift prick up one ear and dart into the cave.

For a moment Emily was frozen to the spot, not knowing what to do. She knew they should run and hide before the kidnappers came rushing out to see where the dog had come from. But she couldn't leave Drift! She had to go in after him. She grabbed a torch from her bag, took a deep breath and stepped into the cave.

'Where are you going?' Jack demanded.

'I've got to help Drift,' Emily snapped defiantly. 'You can't stop me!'

'Not without me you're not!' Jack pulled his torch from his backpack.

Scott was about to warn Jack and Emily about the dangers of walking into the kidnappers' lair, but it was too late. They were already inside. He had no option but to follow.

Feeling her way along the wall, Emily tiptoed inside. At first she could see her way by the light pouring in through the mouth of the cave. They were in a narrow passageway, with barely enough headroom to stand up. As they ventured further in, the walls grew damper and the light dwindled. Emily knew that soon they would have to switch on their torches and risk the kidnappers seeing the lights. She stopped to listen. Water dripping from the ceiling echoed around the walls and up ahead she thought she heard a soft slurping noise she recognized as . . .

'Aggggggghhhhhh!'

Emily's heart almost burst out of her chest as Jack screamed in her ear. She jumped, hit her head on the rock, switched on her torch and swung round. Dazzled by the spotlight, Jack shrank back against the wall.

'What happened?' Emily hissed, looking everywhere for the cause of Jack's freak-out.

Jack blinked and rubbed his neck. 'Massive drop of water right down the back of my t-shirt.'

'You total *dork*!' Scott fumed. 'We thought you'd been attacked.'

'It was *freezing*!' Jack protested.

'At least now we know the kidnappers aren't in here,' Emily sighed. 'They could hardly have missed that!'

Scott stomped ahead shining his torch around like a laser show. There was no point even *trying* to be hush-hush now that Jack 'Stealth Mode' Carter had announced their arrival to anyone within a twenty-mile radius. He might as well have hired a samba band and a troupe of dancing elephants to complete the effect.

The cave widened out into a small room. Scott stepped inside and almost screamed in terror himself. In the yellow beam of his torch, the figures of a ferocious wolf and a cave troll were projected against the back wall. Slowly Scott lowered the torch. His knees almost gave way with relief! The wolf-shadow belonged to Drift. The troll was a teenage boy.

The boy huddled on a sleeping bag in the corner with Drift licking his hand. His face was streaked with grime and his brown hair was lank with grease, but Scott recognized the boy he'd seen playing football with Harry and Jamal.

'Prince Sebastian, I presume,' Scott said, remembering a line from an old movie.

The boy shielded his eyes against the torch beam and shook his head.

Emily entered the chamber. 'Or should we use your English name? Sam Chambers.'

'You're mistaken,' the boy said. 'I am a local fisherman and I've come into this cave to rest. Now, would you be so kind as to leave me in peace?'

If you're a local fisherman, I'm Paddington Bear! Jack thought. The boy's voice was so posh he sounded more like Prince Charles!

Emily wedged her torch in a cranny in the wall and knelt next to Drift at the boy's side. 'We need to work quickly to get you out of here before the NMF kidnappers come back,' she told him urgently.

'You know your so-called best buddy, Jamal, is working for them, don't you?' Jack chipped in.

The boy's eyes widened. 'No!' he spluttered. 'It's not true!'

Jack nodded. ''Fraid so.'

'Never mind that!' Emily said, grabbing the boy's arm. 'How many agents are there? What weapons are they carrying? When did they—'

The boy cowered and snatched his arm away as if

Emily might bite. 'I don't know who you three are but you must have suffered a touch of sunstroke.'

Meanwhile Scott was getting more and more twitchy. The kidnappers could leap out of the shadows at any moment, tie them up, gag them and . . . he didn't even want to think about the rest. They had to get out of here. 'Fine!' he snapped. 'If you don't *want* to be rescued we'll just go home.'

But Jack had thought of a way to snap Sam out of his idiotic 'local fisherman' act. He gently scooped Boz from his shorts pocket and held out his hand. With his fingers curled around the soft body, feeling the pitter-patter heartbeat and the nudge of the damp little nose against his palm, Jack hesitated. He could hardly bear to hand his trusty teammate over to this stuck-up weirdo, but it had to be done. Sam was the rightful owner. He opened his hand. 'I've been looking after him for you.'

The boy stared at the white mouse on Jack's palm. '*Him?* She's not a . . .' He tried to bite back the words but it was too late. Realizing he'd given the game away Sam pushed a hank of greasy hair out of his eyes and smiled weakly. 'Yes, you're right. She's mine. Come on, Pasca,' he coaxed.

Boz glanced up at Jack as if to say goodbye. Then he (or she) hopped into Sam's outstretched hand. Sam's eyes welled with tears as he lifted the mouse to his lips and kissed the pale pink ears. 'Where did you find her?'

'Bosgoose Cottage,' Jack sniffed back a tear of his own.

The boy slumped against the cave wall. After a moment he seemed to come to a decision. 'OK. I'll admit it. Yes, I am Sam Chambers. Or rather, Prince Sebastian, and yes, I have been kidnapped by the New Medania Faction.'

'So where are they now?' Scott asked.

'They went off. In a boat. They said they would return soon.'

'Why didn't they tie you up?' Emily demanded.

Sam looked away to avoid Emily's gaze. 'No need. I can't go anywhere. The kidnappers were terribly rough and I slipped on the rocks when they manhandled me in here. My leg is so swollen I can hardly walk.' He gestured at a mottled yellow-green bruise on his shin.

'We'll soon sort that out,' Emily said. She found an instant ice pack in the first aid kit in her backpack, broke the seal and slapped it onto the bruise.

That proves it! she thought. She'd been pretty sure already but *now* she was certain.

Sam was still lying!

It wasn't just that his eyes had constantly flicked to the right while he talked about the kidnappers. Or that there was only one set of footprints on the beach. The real clincher had been his reaction when she'd walloped the ice pack onto his shin. Or rather the lack of it! *He hadn't even flinched.* Either he had an incredibly high pain threshold or that leg wasn't as badly injured as he was making out. In which case, why hadn't he tried to get away before the kidnappers came back?

Suddenly Emily remembered one tiny detail and everything clicked into place.

It was something that Mrs McElroy in the mini-market had said. *The missing boy was the only one who showed any interest in Castle Key . . .*

Emily narrowed her eyes at Sam. 'The kidnappers aren't *going* to come back, are they?' She paused to let her words sink in, before answering her own question, '*Because there aren't any kidnappers.*'

Jack gaped at her. 'So who was Jamal signalling?'

Emily kept her gaze fixed on Sam. 'It was you, wasn't it? You staged the whole thing and Jamal has been helping you.'

A series of expressions battled for control of Sam's face. First he scowled and started to deny everything. Then he attempted to laugh it off. Finally, he held his hands up in surrender. 'It's true,' he said. His jaw unclenched with the relief of dropping the pretence at last. Without the scowl he suddenly looked like a much nicer person.

Scott was just as relieved. *No kidnappers!* They weren't going to be bound and gagged after all. 'Why don't we get out of this gloomy cave and make camp?' he suggested.

'And break open the provisions,' Jack agreed. It was well past dinnertime.

Sam frowned. 'But I mustn't be seen.'

'Don't worry,' Scott said. 'Nobody's looking for you any more. They think you're in London.'

'We'll build a shelter and catch some fish.' In the torchlight, Emily's dark eyes sparkled with excitement. 'And while they're cooking, Sam can tell us the whole story!'

Sam jumped to his feet. 'It's a deal!' He held out his hand for a formal handshake.

Scott shook his hand. 'I'm Scott. You've met Drift, of course. This is my brother, Jack.'

Jack held up his hand for a high-five. Sam grinned and slapped palms. 'Thank you for looking after Pasca for me.'

'And this is Emily,' Scott said.

'Enchanted to meet you.' Sam bowed, took Emily's hand and made as if to kiss it.

Emily pulled away in shock. 'Yeah, you too!' she gabbled.

'Let me take that for you,' Sam offered, holding out his arm for her backpack.

'I *am* capable of carrying my own kit, thank you,' Emily said stiffly. But as she turned and led the way out of the cave she was smiling. Not that it was anything to do with Sam's Prince Charming act, of course. The baffling mystery was almost solved and she had a camp to set up.

This was turning out to be Emily's dream trip!

Nineteen

Survival Camp

Sam and Jack were in charge of building a shelter, while Emily, Scott and Drift went hunting and gathering. First they filled flasks with water from shallow pools in the rocks – visiting only ones above the tideline that had collected rain rather than salt water. The water looked a little green and soupy but Emily insisted that it would be fine once she'd added the water purification tablets from her survival kit. Scott wasn't so sure. Now the water was green, soupy *and* had the taste of pine-fresh Toilet Duck.

Next they fished for their supper. They attached fishing line (also from Emily's survival kit) to rods made from long sticks, and then baited hooks fashioned from shards of shell with pieces of dead crab gathered from the beach. They climbed onto the rocks and cast their lines into the sea.

An hour later the sun was sinking in the west and they had caught nothing but two small dogfish with freckled grey skin and sharkish grins.

As she and Scott trailed back along the beach Emily had to admit the fishing hadn't gone quite as well as she'd hoped. But she cheered up again when she spotted a mass of seaweed.

'Bladderwrack is edible,' she told Scott. 'It'll be perfect with the dogfish.'

Scott looked at the muddy green fronds covered with what looked like large boils. 'Yum yum,' he said faintly. He was starting to wonder whether Jack would trade his tin of Whiskas!

Meanwhile Jack and Sam had finished the shelter in record time.

They'd picked a spot on the beach where a circle of shoulder-high rocks formed a small fort with one side open to the sea. They piled gorse branches over the top to form a sort of thatched roof. Then they cushioned the floor with clumps of heather. Sam even insisted on screening off a separate sleeping area for Emily, which he furnished with blankets and his video player (complete with battery pack) from his cave, and bunches of wild daisies and poppies.

Jack laughed. 'What are you doing?'

'Making it look ladylike,' Sam said.

'*Ladylike?*' Jack snorted. 'You've not actually *met* many girls, have you?'

'Of course I have. We have two social events with Braithwaite Girls' School every year.'

Then again, Jack thought, *it wouldn't help if Sam were best friends with the entire female population of the planet.* Emily Wild wasn't exactly your average girl!

By the time Emily, Scott and Drift returned, Jack and Sam had built a campfire and were investigating Sam's food store.

'Wow!' Jack laughed, burrowing into the huge basket. 'Looks like you've got half of Harrods Food Hall in here!' He helped himself to some salami and cheese and a bottle of Perrier water. 'Can I tempt anyone with a little smoked salmon?' he asked.

Emily looked up from skinning and gutting the dogfish. 'No, thank you! *Some of us* are practising our survival skills. Aren't we, Scott?'

'May I help you with those fish?' Sam offered.

Emily brandished her blood-spattered penknife. 'I can manage perfectly well, thank you.'

Scott looked longingly at the smoked salmon, but he

placed a pot of chlorine-smelling water on the fire and chucked in a handful of bladderwrack.

Sam pulled a large piece of driftwood up to the fire and sat down. 'So how did you guys know that I hadn't really been kidnapped?' he asked.

Yeah, good question! Jack thought. He'd been wondering the same thing. 'I think we'll let Emily explain,' he bluffed. 'Ladies first, eh?'

Emily stuck her tongue out at Jack. She hated being called a lady. On the other hand, she *loved* showing off her detective skills. 'It was Mrs McElroy in the mini-market who provided the vital clue.'

'Exactly!' Jack tried to look as if he knew what Emily was talking about.

'Mrs McElroy told us that the missing boy was interested in Castle Key,' Emily went on, as she speared the fish with sticks and stuck them into the sand so that the fish were held at an angle over the flames. 'She said that you even bought a guidebook. One exactly like this, I believe?' Emily pulled out her own copy of *Discover Castle Key* and held it up.

Sam stared at the guidebook and nodded.

Emily was really enjoying herself now. She took her time stirring the seaweed, knowing the three boys were hanging on her every word. 'It has maps of the island and tide tables – which you needed to find a suitable hiding place for when you went missing. First you considered Bosgoose Cottage . . .'

'That's right,' Sam said. 'It says in the book that people keep away from there because of some legend about an old woman stealing children. I thought it sounded ideal so we checked it out, but then I saw that someone had been there recently – there was a bit of half-eaten banana cake – so I decided it wasn't safe.'

'Yeah, that was us!' Jack laughed. 'So that must be when you lost Boz, sorry, *Pasca*.'

Sam looked down at the little mouse perched on his knee. 'I realized she'd gone when I got back to camp but I didn't have time to go back for her, so Jamal promised he'd try and find her. I'd read in the guidebook about Black Rock Island and I knew this would be the perfect place. I sneaked out of the camp in the middle of the night and came across the causeway at low tide. Jamal helped me bring enough supplies to last a week or two if necessary . . .'

'Now I know why Jamal didn't seem too bothered that his best friend was missing,' Jack said. 'He knew you were safely holed up here.'

Sam nodded. 'He also agreed to invent some "suspicious men" to make it look like a real kidnap.'

'We figured out he was lying,' Emily said. 'Eventually.'

'Eventually?' Jack laughed. 'I was on to him straight away!'

Emily and Scott both rolled their eyes. The conversation paused as Emily served food onto plates made of flat stones. Scott felt he had to take some. Sam was too polite to refuse.

Jack, on the other hand, took one look at the charred lumps of dogfish on their bed of alien slime and reached into the Harrods hamper instead. 'Think I'll stick to parma ham and a selection of fine cheeses!'

Scott nibbled at the seaweed and almost choked. To call bladderwrack *edible* was using the word in its very loosest sense. It was *edible* in the same way that an old boot was edible. You *could* eat it, but nobody in their right mind would choose to. 'So, come on, Sam,' he spluttered. 'You've told us how you staged your own kidnap. Now tell us *why*.'

Sam poked the fire with a stick, sending a fountain of orange sparks leaping into the darkness. Night had gathered round them as they sat talking. 'Just before coming to Castle Key, I received a message from the royal advisors in Medania to inform me that my uncle, King Orlando, is very ill. He's not expected to live more than a few months.'

'I'm very sorry,' Scott said sympathetically.

'Actually, I don't know my uncle very well. My parents were both killed in a plane crash when I was five. I've been at boarding school ever since.' Sam stared into the flames. Scott, Jack and Emily waited for him to continue the story in his own time. There was no hurry. It was a warm night and they had plenty of driftwood for the fire.

Sam took a bite of dogfish and quickly put his plate down. 'The royal advisors said that as soon as I got back from Castle Key, they were coming to Braithwaite to take me home to Medania. I'm the heir to the throne and they want to start preparing me to take over after Uncle Orlando dies.'

Jack whistled. 'You're going to be a king? How cool is that!'

Sam pulled a face. 'Not cool at all! All those boring royal duties like meeting politicians and opening new hospitals! I'd have bodyguards following me everywhere. I'd never have any freedom. There'd be none of *this* . . .' He swept his arm in a gesture that included Scott, Jack and Emily, their faces aglow in the campfire light, Drift snoozing on the warm sand, the sheltering rocks, the gently lapping waves, the lights of the fishing boats in the distance and the millions upon millions of stars that studded the sky like sequins on black velvet.

Jack breathed in a lungful of air fragrant with sea salt and wood smoke and sighed. 'I guess, when you put it like that, being king's not as great as it's cracked up to be.'

'That's not even the worst of it,' Sam said. 'They'd marry me off to some spoiled princess with a servant just to brush her hair.' He glanced at Emily whose tangle of chestnut curls curtained her face as she whittled a toasting stick with her penknife. She'd finally relented and agreed to share the marshmallows that Jack had brought from Stone Cottage. 'And my dreams of being a professional football player would all be over, of course.'

Scott lay back on the sand and gazed up at the stars. That was one of his dreams too. He knew how he'd feel if it was taken away from him. 'Yeah, Jamal and Harry told us you'd been scouted by Arsenal.' He sat up and grinned. 'Shame you couldn't find a *decent* team!'

Sam laughed. 'Like what?'

'Chelsea, of course!'

'Chelsea? I want to play *football*, remember!'

Scott fired a marshmallow at Sam. Their laughter rang out on the still night air.

'So you decided to stage this kidnap so you don't have to be king?' Emily said.

Sam nodded.

'But what about the ransom note?' Jack asked.

'It was a fake,' Sam explained. 'I recruited the help of my sister, Sasha. She's still in Medania. She sent the ransom note pretending it was from the NMF and demanding that Uncle Orlando sign an agreement to hand the crown over to our cousin, Ferdinand. The NMF's been campaigning for that for years, so everyone believed it was genuine.'

Scott had to admire Sam's attention to detail. 'And you told her to say in the note that the NMF had taken you to London so people would stop searching for you here in Castle Key.'

'That's right. I'm going to lie low here for a few days then make my way to the mainland. As soon as Ferdinand's safely on the throne, I can "reappear" without any fear of having to go back and be king.'

'But what will you live on?' Jack asked. 'That Harrods hamper won't last forever.'

'Sasha will send me money. When the fuss has died down I'll go back to London. If I'm lucky I'll get signed up by one of the football clubs and start earning my own money . . .'

The friends sat for a while longer gazing into the flames. They were all yawning. Jack could hardly keep his eyes open. 'Got to get some kip . . . g'night!' he mumbled eventually as he crawled into the shelter.

Scott remembered to send a text message to Old Bob on his fishing boat nearby to say that all was well. Then he followed Jack.

'Don't worry. We'll help you get back to London,' Emily told Sam as she tipped sand on the fire to put it out.

Jack was just drifting off to sleep on his pillow of heather when he heard a commotion from the 'girl's quarters'. 'What's all this stuff?' Emily was muttering. 'This is a survival camp, not a five-star hotel!'

Blankets and gadgets began tumbling over the partition.

Jack noticed she didn't throw the flowers out though.

Twenty

Unwelcome Arrivals

The four friends spent the next day exploring the island, searching the rock pools for mussels and making improvements to their shelter, all the while working on their plan to help Sam escape. They would all stay on Black Rock Island for two more nights, they decided, until the search for Sam had completely died down. On the third night, they would sneak back over the causeway under cover of darkness and go to

Stone Cottage. Sam would borrow Scott's bike, cycle to Carrickstowe Station and catch the first train to London – leaving the bike locked up at the station for Scott to collect later.

They were sitting on a small rocky beach on the north shore of the island, drying off in the sunshine after an afternoon swim, when Drift flicked his ears into Listening Formation.

A few moments later the humans could hear it too: a small powerboat skipping its way across the waves from Castle Key island.

Sam turned to the others, his eyes wide with fear.

Scott looked up from carving a fishing float from a piece of driftwood. 'Probably just holidaymakers out for a spin.'

Emily took her binoculars from her bag and zoomed in on the boat.

It wasn't holidaymakers.

There were two men on deck, both in black t-shirts and camo-pattern trousers. A third figure sat slumped with his head in his hands . . .

Emily took in the cropped black hair, the dark brown skin . . . 'It's Jamal!' she breathed.

One of the men on the boat reached for the binoculars hanging round his neck.

'Quick! Hide!' Emily shouted.

Scott, Jack, Sam, Emily and Drift threw themselves behind the rocks. Just in time! When Emily peeped out, the man in the boat had his binoculars pointed directly at Black Rock Island.

'Let me look!' Forgetting his manners for once, Sam snatched the binoculars. 'Oh, no!' he groaned. 'I recognize those men. They're two of the leaders of the New Medania Faction.'

'What?' Jack asked. 'They've kidnapped *Jamal* now? Is *he* in line to be King of Medania as well?'

'They must have heard about the ransom note that was meant to be from the NMF,' Sam said in a grim voice. 'Of course, they know *they* haven't kidnapped me, so I guess they've come to find out what's going on. They must have got hold of Jamal and forced him to tell them where I am.'

'What will they do if they catch you?' Scott asked.

Sam was still staring through the binoculars. 'I guess they'll use me as a bargaining tool to get Uncle Orlando to hand over the crown to Ferdinand – just like in my fake ransom note.' Sam slowly lowered the binoculars. 'Which would be fine if they stopped there, but the NMF are ruthless. I don't trust them. They'll probably demand millions of pounds as well!' He laughed bitterly. 'And, knowing them, they'll wait until they have what they want, then kill me anyway.'

The friends fell silent. The drone of the motor grew louder as the speedboat closed in.

Sam handed the binoculars back to Emily and stood up.

'What are you doing?' Jack hissed, yanking him back down by his t-shirt.

'I have to give myself up in exchange for Jamal.'

Scott frowned. 'But you said they'd probably kill you!'

'If they don't have me they'll take it out on Jamal.' Sam pulled away from Jack's grasp. 'This is my battle, not Jamal's.' He turned back and gave a brave smile. 'Thanks for everything. Stay here and don't let them see you.'

'No!' Emily cried. The boat was already scraping noisily onto the shingle at the far end of the beach. 'There has to be *something* we can do!'

'There is!' Scott said. He'd just had a brilliant idea. 'You guys stay hidden. I'll go out and pretend to be Sam, but I'll run off before they can capture me. While they're chasing me round the island, you untie Jamal and get the boat ready to leave. I'll give the men the slip and then join you.'

Sam shook his head. 'Too risky. What if they catch you?'

'Then they'll soon realize I'm not Prince Sebastian and let me go. But they *won't* catch me! We've spent all morning exploring the maze through the rocks – I can find *my* way and make sure they lose *theirs*.'

Emily thought for a moment. *It might work!* Scott and Sam were the same height and build. They both had grey eyes and floppy brown hair. They were both wearing faded t-shirts and baggy shorts.

Sam clapped Scott on the shoulder. 'It's a good plan,' he agreed, 'but with one change – I'll be the one to lead them off on the chase. That way you'll all still be safe if they catch me.'

But it was too late. Scott had already stepped out from behind the rocks to meet the two men, who were now dragging Jamal along the beach between them.

Jamal's wrists and ankles were bound with ropes. When he heard Scott's footsteps he hung his head as if he couldn't face the friend he had betrayed. 'I'm s-s-sorry, Sam,' he sobbed. 'They were waiting for me when we got back to Braithwaite School last night. I didn't want to tell them you were here, but they *forced* me. They threatened my family.'

Scott stopped a short distance from the men and their prisoner. 'Don't worry, Jamal. I understand.'

Jamal's head jerked up. Scott's attempt to imitate Sam's voice hadn't fooled him. 'But you're not . . .'

'No!' Scott shouted over him. 'I'm *not . . . angry* with you!' He shook his head desperately at Jamal, willing him not to give the game away.

One of the men yelled something at Scott.

Scott didn't understand a word of it. For a moment he was stumped. How could he pass himself off as Prince Sebastian if he couldn't speak Medanian? But then he remembered. He did know *one* word of Medanian. He glared at the NMF men and hurled that word at them

171

with all the venom he could muster, '*Chanko!*'

The men looked at each other and then back at Scott, their faces like thunder. They were outraged at being called rats! They began shouting back at him. Scott didn't wait to hear more. With a last cry of *Chanko!* he sprinted down the beach, leaping over heaps of seaweed and weaving through the rocks. He could hear footsteps pounding along behind him. *The plan was working!*

When he reached the end of the beach Scott glanced over his shoulder. The men were gaining on him fast. He clambered up a bank of rock, then doubled back through a tunnel and squeezed through a hidden gap that led towards a narrow ravine . . . all he could do was keep going.

Meanwhile, Emily, Drift, Jack and Sam ran to Jamal's side. The NMF men had shoved him roughly to the ground and left him there, trussed up like a Christmas turkey.

'What?' Jamal spluttered, fighting against the ropes. 'How?'

'We'll explain later!' Jack said.

Emily and Sam took their penknives from their pockets and began hacking through the ropes.

'Stop wriggling!' Sam told Jamal. 'We want to cut you free, not slice you to pieces.'

'I'll get the boat ready,' Jack cried. He sprinted off along the beach with Drift flying along at his heels. He saw Scott emerge from a gap in the rocks up ahead and come running towards him. He looked back over his shoulder. Sam, Emily and Jamal – now free of his ropes – weren't far behind, jogging to catch up with him.

The plan was working brilliantly. They just needed to get in . . .

'The boat!' Jack gasped, staring at the spot where the boat had been sitting moments before.

The boat was gone.

Twenty-one

Trapped!

Jack looked up to see the small speedboat drifting away. The men hadn't pulled it far enough up onto the beach! He waded into the water after it, but just as he reached out to grab the bow, the boat was swept up by a huge wave and pitched onto a jagged rock, which tore a gash in the hull and then flung it further out to sea. Jack picked himself up and turned to see Scott, Sam, Emily, Jamal and Drift gathered on the beach, all staring at the stricken boat disappearing into the distance.

'So what's Plan B?' Jack asked, trying to keep the panic out of his voice.

'I'll send Old Bob a message,' Scott suggested, grabbing his phone and frantically typing.

Emily chewed her lip. 'OK, but it could take him twenty minutes to get here and those guys'll be back any second. We'll have to cross over the causeway.'

'But low tide was over two hours ago!' Sam said. 'It'll be too far underwater by now.'

'It'll be about this deep.' Emily indicated her chest. 'We can do it.'

'Can't we just swim, anyway?' Sam asked.

But Emily shook her head. 'No, when the water gets too deep there's a nasty current that can drag you under. We need to stick together and stay on the sandbar.'

Scott glanced inland. He thought he could hear someone moving. 'OK. It's our only chance.'

Without another word the friends all scrambled over the rocks to the next cove, where the causeway joined the island.

'We'll never find it!' Jack groaned, looking out over the expanse of water towards Chicken Bay. So near and yet so far, and the tide was coming in all the time, the waves getting deeper and deeper. The thought of that current dragging him down to the depths was making his stomach churn.

Scott ran to the water's edge and looked up at the

rocks behind him. 'I'm sure it comes out just beneath this ridge of rock. It's where I thought the kidnappers would be waiting to ambush us when we crossed yesterday.'

They all waded into the water, feeling around with their feet for the sandbar.

After a few moments Jack stumbled across it. 'It's here!' he called.

Scott, Emily, Drift, Sam and Jamal hurried to his side.

'We head directly for the chicken's beak,' Emily said, pointing to the rock formation on the cliffs across the narrow channel. Then she picked Drift up and began to walk out to sea.

Sam pulled her back. 'I'll take Drift for you.'

But Scott stepped in front of him and scooped Drift out of Emily's arms.

'What about Boz?' Jack cried.

'It's OK,' Sam said, taking the mouse from his pocket and placing her on his head where she clung to his hair.

Together the five friends forged through the choppy waves. Up to their chests, holding each other up when they were knocked off balance by a large wave or pulled over by the bullying current that tugged at their legs, they half waded, half swam for shore. As the shortest and lightest, Emily choked and spluttered as wave after wave washed her off her feet, but she fixed her gaze on the chicken's beak and forced herself on. Then she felt a hand on her arm.

'Piggy back?' Jamal offered.

Emily was about to tell him she didn't need help when another breaker crashed over her head, filling her mouth and nostrils with salt water yet again. 'Thanks!' she said, hopping up onto Jamal's broad back.

Just then, Emily heard a shout and looked back over her shoulder. The two men were standing in the cove at Black Rock Island, waving their arms and yelling in Medanian.

'Oh, no, they're coming after us!' Scott said, turning and walking backwards to look. His arms were in agony from holding Drift up and they were all slowing down from the effort of walking through the deep water.

Jack made the mistake of looking back. The men were wading along the causeway behind them. Taller and stronger, they were gaining fast! He tried to speed up, but all of a sudden he was sideswiped by a massive wave and lost his footing. Gripped by panic, Jack thrashed his legs, frantically trying to make contact with the sandbank, but there was nothing but water sucking him down, water rushing into his nose and mouth, water filling his lungs . . .

Just when Jack thought it was all over, he felt a hand grab his arm and pull him back.

'Come on!' Sam shouted. 'We're almost there.'

Jack clung on and let himself be dragged along. At last, he realized the water was getting shallower. They'd made it!

The friends stumbled onto the beach and threw themselves gasping and spluttering onto dry land.

'Come on,' Scott said, pulling Jack up. 'We can't stop here. They'll catch us up any minute.' He looked back across the water to see the two men already halfway across the channel. But suddenly an enormous wave broke with a boom and a fountain of spray, flinging the men far from the causeway to land in the frothing tumult of open water.

'We'll have to try and help them,' Scott cried. 'They'll drown!'

'No, look!' Emily cried. 'Old Bob must have got your message.' They all watched as a familiar green fishing boat came into view from behind Black Rock Island.

'And he's called the coastguard out too!' Jamal laughed, pointing at an orange lifeboat speeding onto the scene.

The friends sat on the beach and watched as the NMF men were thrown life rings and fished out of the waves.

'Safe at last!' Jamal sighed.

They all knew he wasn't just talking about the Medanians!

There was quite a crowd squeezed onto the flower-print sofas and chairs in the living room at Stone Cottage the next morning. Sam and Jamal had stayed the night, and were now sitting with Scott, Jack and Emily, along with Sam's twin sister, Sasha, and an elderly royal advisor. They had flown in from Medania to escort Sam – or rather, Prince Sebastian – home to take up his royal duties. Drift and Boomerang were curled up on the hearth rug.

'Being king won't be so bad, Seb,' Sasha said, smiling gently. She had the same serious grey eyes as her brother, and straight brown hair which she wore in a long plait over one shoulder. She smoothed her elegant white linen dress over her knees. 'I'll help you with the royal duties. I've taken over a lot of them already while Uncle Orlando has been so ill.'

Sam looked at the royal advisor. 'Can't we just let Ferdinand take over? He's a nice guy. He'll make a perfectly good king.'

The royal advisor, an elderly man in a dark grey suit, adjusted his half-moon glasses and twisted the end of his white beard into an even sharper point. He exchanged a glance with Sasha and cleared his throat. 'Certain things have happened while you've been away that you don't understand, Sebastian. Your cousin, Ferdinand, is a *nice* man, as you say. But he's also a weak man. He has run up a mountain of gambling debts. The New Medania Faction has been paying them off for him but, if he were king, he'd almost certainly fritter away all the country's money in the casino. And then it would be the NMF who would have the real power.' The advisor turned to Scott, Jack and Emily. 'You may not have heard of the NMF, but they are a very dangerous group, mainly funded by organized crime – a sort of mafia, you might say.'

Sam turned to Sasha. 'Is all this true?'

Sasha nodded gravely.

Sam puffed out his cheeks and sighed. 'In that case I have no choice. I can't let Medania be ruined by the NMF. I will come home and take the throne.'

Emily swallowed a lump in her throat. It was so unfair!

Just then, Aunt Kate came in to the room with a tray of drinks and cakes. Sam stood up to help her. 'Isn't there *anyone* else in the family who could take Sebastian's place?' Aunt Kate asked, looking over her glasses at Emily. Then she let her eyes drift towards Sasha.

'Of course!' Emily shouted, leaping out of her chair. 'Sasha could do it!' She threw herself at Sasha's knees and held her hands. 'You could take the crown. You've already been helping your uncle. You'd be brilliant!'

Sasha looked uncertainly at the royal advisor. His brow furrowed. 'The crown of Medania has always passed to the male heir . . .'

'Can't Orlando give the crown to anyone he wants?' Scott asked. 'He *is* king, after all.'

The royal advisor stroked his beard. 'Well, we've never had a female monarch in Medania . . . a *queen* . . .'

'We've got one here in England,' Jack pointed out,

'and she's really good at it!'

Jamal grinned. 'And, let's face it, Sasha would look a lot prettier on all the stamps!'

The royal advisor leaned back in his chair. 'It is unprecedented in Medania, but I think it is an excellent idea.' Then he turned to Sasha. 'Would you be prepared to take on this responsibility, my dear?'

Sasha looked down at her hands. When she looked up she was smiling. 'I would be honoured.'

Sam launched himself at his sister and wrapped her in a hug.

Aunt Kate raised her mug of tea. 'A toast! To Queen Sasha!'

Emily grinned as they all chinked their mugs together.

'To football!' Scott added, grinning at Sam. 'May you score many goals – just not against Chelsea!'

Sam laughed. 'I almost forgot. I have some presents for you all.' He turned to Jack and handed him a wooden box with holes punched in the lid.

Jack opened it. A pair of pink eyes looked up at him. 'Boz?' he murmured. 'But, I can't . . .'

'No, this is Rolo,' Sam said. 'He's one of Pasca's many brothers and sisters. I asked Sasha to bring him especially for you.'

Jack stroked Rolo's ears. At last, a pet of his own. 'Awesome!' he said. Then he glanced at Boomerang, pretending to be asleep but in reality keeping a very close eye on the mouse situation. 'Only problem is,' he said. 'I don't think he'd be very safe here.'

Sam looked thoughtful. Then his face brightened. 'That's OK,' he said. 'I'll be staying in England now, so I'll look after him with Pasca for you whenever you're in Castle Key. You can pick him up when you go back to London.'

Jack grinned. Having a pet to go back to would make leaving Castle Key at the end of the summer so much easier. School could be quite bearable with a white mouse in your pocket . . .

Sam handed Scott a large white envelope.

'Season tickets for Chelsea!' Scott laughed when he opened it. 'How did you wangle these?'

Sam grinned. 'Let's just say that having royal connections can come in useful now and then.'

There was a smart new collar for Drift and, last of all, Sam turned to Emily. He leaned across the coffee table and presented her with a tiny gold box.

Oh, no! Jack thought. *Prince Charming's only gone and given her something 'ladylike'. This is going to be hilarious!* Jack and Scott craned forward in their chairs, eager to witness the look on Emily's face when she saw a sparkly necklace or earrings. But to their astonishment, as Emily opened the lid her face lit up with a million-watt smile.

'Wow!' she breathed as she stared into the box. 'Thank you! This is *so* cool!'

Jack and Scott couldn't bear the suspense. They

jumped up and hung over the back of Emily's chair to see what had impressed her so much. A whopping great diamond? A ruby-encrusted tiara?

Resting on a cushion of purple satin was a small silver badge. A coat of arms in the middle was encircled by the words *Medanian Secret Service – Honorary Member*. Inside the lid of the box were engraved the words, *Presented to Emily Wild in recognition of outstanding services to the Principality of Medania*.

The royal advisor smiled at Emily. 'We have made this award on the personal recommendation of one of our top agents. I believe you've met Anya? Not her real name, of course. She was most impressed with your surveillance and combat skills—'

'Even if she did think you were spying for the NMF!' Sasha laughed.

———

After all the guests had left, Scott, Jack and Emily climbed up to the treehouse and hoisted Drift up in his basket-lift.

Emily opened *Discover Castle Key* and began to check the tide tables. It was the copy from Aunt Kate's bookshelf. Emily's copy had been left behind on Black Rock Island in her bag, along with all their backpacks. 'We'll have to go over this afternoon and pick up our stuff,' she said. 'In fact, why don't we stay there for a few more nights? It would be a shame to waste that amazing shelter we made.'

Jack looked up from the hammock where he was dreaming up new tricks to teach Rolo when he got back to London. He was sure that owning a mouse would open up a whole new armoury of school pranks too. 'OK. On one condition.'

'What?' Emily asked.

Jack grinned. 'You let me be in charge of food supplies!'

Scott raised his hand. 'I never thought I'd say this but Jack definitely gets my vote on this one.'

Emily was about to object, but she suddenly found herself smiling. 'OK. I admit it! That seaweed was *disgusting*!'

'Nearly as bad as the dogfish!' Scott said.

They all laughed.

'And you never know,' Jack added. 'We might just come across another mystery while we're there . . .'

Author's Note

Don't worry if you can't find Medania on a map of Europe. The small country was invented for the purposes of this story, as was the New Medania Faction.

The information about the four-letter International Civil Aviation Organisation codes for airports is true: EGLL really is the code for London Heathrow. However, for the fictional airport in Medania, I borrowed the country code for the island of Malta.

Don't miss the next exciting mystery in the
Adventure Island series

THE MYSTERY
OF THE BLACK SALAMANDER

Available now!

Read on for a special preview
of the first chapters.

One

Exciting News

It was a high-risk mission but Jack Carter knew he could handle it. He had a priceless cargo to deliver. And he had to move fast. The payload was extremely unstable. In this heat, total meltdown could happen at any second.

Sweat ran into his eyes. Jack blinked it away. He gauged the distance to the exit. His knuckles tightened as he gripped the tray. He turned from the counter and struck out across no man's land, the James Bond theme playing in his head. A tricky little backward shimmy through the door in the slipstream of a departing customer and he was out.

Mission accomplished!

'One strawberry sundae,' he said, handing a tall glass of ice cream to his brother, who was sitting in the shade of a striped parasol, squinting at his iPod screen.

'And, for me, choco-banoffee-marshmallow-cookie-dough ice cream with extra whipped cream, rainbow sprinkles and caramel sauce.' Jack stood back to admire the spectacular creation.

Scott pulled a face. 'That looks gross!'

Jack frowned. 'You're right! It's definitely missing something.' He headed back into Dotty's Tea Rooms. A moment later he emerged from the café and placed a shiny red cherry on the top. 'There! A work of art!'

It was one of those hot, sticky days when the sky bulged with purple clouds, and little black thunderbugs flew into your hair and – for reasons known only to themselves – tried to crawl up your nose. Jack and Scott had spent the morning helping Aunt Kate in the garden at Stone Cottage. Ever since their first visit to Castle Key last summer, when they'd met Emily Wild and solved the mystery of the whistling caves, they'd come to stay with their aunt – technically their *great*-aunt – every school holiday, while their dad was off travelling the world on archaeological digs. Their mum had died in a car accident when Jack was so little that he wasn't sure whether his memories of her were real, or whether he was just remembering the faded photos in the old albums.

Looking up from his ice cream Jack saw Emily bombing along the seafront on her bike. She was standing up on the pedals, her long brown curls streaming out behind her. She skidded to a halt, her front tyre bumping the edge of the table. Drift hopped down from his special basket on the back, wagging his tail in bliss. After his beloved Emily, Jack and Scott were his all-time favourite humans. *And* they had ice cream!

'Exciting news ...' Emily panted. 'I've just heard ...'

Jack and Scott exchanged grins. Knowing Emily, she'd uncovered a smuggling ring, a treasure map or, at the very least, a plot to steal the Crown Jewels.

'... from the Castle Key Nature Watch Group!' Emily went on.

Nature Group? A lump of ice cream slithered down Jack's gullet. He hadn't felt this disappointed since his last birthday present from Gran turned out to be a pair of socks. He wouldn't have minded so much, but they'd been pink with ballerinas all over them.

Jack had nothing against nature. He liked animals. He loved Drift, of course, and Aunt Kate's tabby kitten, Boomerang. And during their last case he'd even been appointed by the Carrickstowe police as official guardian to the Prince of Medania's white mouse (long story!). But as far as Jack was concerned, nature didn't like *him;* it was always biting him, stinging him or crawling up his nose. He was sure a couple of those thunderbugs were still camping out inside his right nostril. *And don't even get me started on spiders,* he thought.

Emily helped herself to a spoonful of Jack's ice cream. 'We're talking *killer whales*!' she said dramatically.

Suddenly Jack was interested. Killer whales were *serious* wildlife, like tigers and polar bears: the kind of nature you saw on TV programmes.

'I didn't know there were orcas in Cornwall,' Scott said.

Jack snorted – not a wise move with a nose full of thunderbugs and a mouthful of ice cream. *Typical of Scott 'Know-it-All' Carter to show off by using the scientific name,* he thought.

'It's very rare to see them here,' Emily agreed, 'but two were spotted off North Point this morning. You guys coming to see?'

—

The friends cycled out of Castle Key village, over the common and along the track across North Moor. It was a wild and remote corner of the island. A few sheep meandered among clumps of gorse and heather cropping the short, springy grass. Seagulls wailed high overhead. The only signs that humans had ever passed this way were the abandoned tin mine and the ancient standing stones.

But that all changed when they reached the coast. A small crowd had gathered on North Point, a craggy promontory where huge boulders were stacked in tumbling heaps and strewn around like giant Jenga blocks.

Everyone was staring out across the water. Some had obviously settled in for the day, with folding chairs and flasks of tea. Emily took the binoculars from the investigation kit she always carried in her shoulder bag. She looked for a moment, shook her head and handed them to Jack. He scanned the sea for a pair of jet-black dorsal fins knifing through the water. He could see fishing boats and seagulls, and the buildings on the mainland a mile or so across the channel, but not a single fin.

A man with a disorganized sandy beard and sideburns and a clipboard pressed to his *Save the Rainforest* t-shirt broke away from the crowd. 'Super! Super! Some new young members for the Nature Watch Group. That's what I like to see.' He shook hands all round and introduced himself as Don Penrose. 'We think a mother and a calf must have strayed from their pod and got lost.'

'Maybe they've swum back out to sea,' Scott said. 'Don't they have to come up to breathe every few minutes?'

Don Penrose nodded. 'That's right. We'll keep watching in case they haven't found their way out of the channel.' He thrust his clipboard at the friends. 'Great to have you on board!' Before they knew what was happening, they'd all filled out application forms and signed up to the Castle Key Nature Watch Group.

'Super! I'll put you three down for the early watch on Wednesday, shall I?' Penrose enthused as he handed them each a member's badge. 'Report at six a.m. sharp.'

As they left, Jack shook his head in disbelief. Had he really just joined a nature group? As he picked up his bike he felt something plop on his head. Great! A welcome message from a low-flying seagull!

They were halfway across North Moor when he felt another plop. Then another. But this time it wasn't gulls. There was a rumble of thunder. Diagonal rain came sweeping across the moors and most of it seemed to find its way down the back of Jack's t-shirt.

'Nature!' he groaned. 'Don't you just love it!'

—

Next morning, Scott was woken by the *Match of the Day* ringtone on his phone. He peered at the screen. 'It's Emily!' he muttered.

'Tell me it's not another urgent communication from the Nature Watch Group,' Jack grumbled from under his quilt on the other side of the cosy attic bedroom. 'What is it this time? A herd of invisible rhinos stampeding across the common?'

Scott had the phone to his ear now. 'She says do we want to go and see the black salamander . . .'

'*Salamander?* Isn't that some kind of lizard?' Jack said. 'I think I'll pass.'

But Scott was pushing himself up on his elbows. 'She's talking about *the* Black Salamander!'

Jack sat up so fast he cracked his head on the sloping ceiling. 'No way! That awesome new supercar they were talking about on *Top Gear* the other day? The one with bazillions of cool gadgets? The one that can dive underwater like a submarine?'

Scott could hardly speak for excitement.

He didn't need to.

A single nod of the head said it all!

Two

The Coolest Car on the Planet

As they jumped on their bikes, one super-sized question kept whizzing round Scott's head: how had Emily wangled the chance to see the world's most talked-about supercar? The Black Salamander was so exclusive that only one prototype had been built. The car magazines and websites had been buzzing with rumours about it for months.

'I had a call from Max Fordham this morning,'

Emily explained, as the boys pulled up to meet her on the high street. 'You remember – from Operation Lost Star?'

Scott and Jack both nodded. Max wasn't the kind of guy you forgot in a hurry. He was an ex-SAS soldier who now worked as a stunt co-ordinator for the film industry. Last summer he'd come to stay at The Lighthouse in Castle Key – which Emily's parents ran as a Bed and Breakfast – while working on location on a movie. When Savannah Shaw, the star of the film, had gone missing, Emily, Jack, Scott and Drift were soon on the case.

'The Black Salamander is going to feature in this new Hollywood movie called *Ocean Force*,' Emily went on. 'Max is designing all the stunts, so he's come to see the car in action at the Wheel Power test track.'

'Wow!' Jack whistled. 'That's just outside Carrickstowe, isn't it? What are we waiting for?'

﹏

The Wheel Power test track was on the site of an old airbase not far from the causeway that crossed the narrow channel from Castle Key island. The friends gazed up at the huge metal gates. High-security mesh fencing was festooned with razor wire and bristled with cameras.

Emily stood on tiptoe to reach the speakerphone and

asked nervously for Max Fordham. The gates creaked open. Feeling very small, she and the boys pushed their bikes into a large compound. The gates clanged shut behind them.

Max strolled out from an ugly, red brick building that looked like part of an old Victorian hospital. With his black t-shirt and combat trousers, he looked as if he might still be on special operations with the army, but his steely blue eyes crinkled as he raised his hands for high-fives all round.

'Do we have a problem, Max?'

They all turned to see a slim woman in a red spotted dress hurrying towards them on skyscraper heels. Her glossy black hair glowed with coppery highlights in the bright sunshine. She spoke with an American accent.

'Not at all,' Max answered. 'Scott, Jack and Emily are friends of mine. I've invited them to see the Salamander.'

The woman pursed her red-glossed lips for a moment, then flashed a dazzling smile. 'I am so loving this,' she said. 'Engaging with young people in the community. That *always* plays well.' She nodded as if agreeing with herself. 'I know! We'll do a photo-shoot with the Salamander.' She looked the friends up and down as if they were dresses in the end-of-season sale. 'Hmm, a pretty face, but we'll need a hairbrush ...' she murmured to Emily. She smiled at Scott. 'Fabulous. Loving that floppy-haired boy band look.' Then she came to Jack, slowly taking in the sticking-up hair, the ketchup-stained t-shirt and the grubby knees. Her smile wobbled, but only for a second. 'Nothing we can't sort out in Photoshop!' With that, she whipped a phone out of her handbag and dashed away, reeling off instructions as she went.

'*Boy band!*' Scott snorted, although he couldn't help a blush creeping over his ears.

'*Hairbrush!*' Emily fumed.

'*Photoshop!*' Jack spluttered.

Max laughed. 'That was Alesha Rahal. She's in charge of publicity for Silverwood Motors – that's the company that makes the Black Salamander. She's quite harmless, just a bit ...'

'Bonkers?' Jack suggested.

'I was going to say *full-on!*'

'Publicity?' Scott asked. 'I thought the Black Salamander was all hush-hush?'

'It has been so far,' Max said. 'Silverwood had to make sure other car companies couldn't copy the design or steal all their cutting-edge technology before it was finished. But now the Salamander is almost ready to roll and they can start showing her off. After the last few performance tests here she'll be whisked off to the Monaco Motor Show to be unveiled in a blaze of glory – then shipped to Hollywood to start filming.'

Max tapped a code into the security pad on the door of the red brick building and ushered the friends inside.

They signed their names at a reception desk and were given visitor passes to hang round their necks. Then they walked out through the other side of the building, past storerooms, garages and workshops, until they came to a racing circuit in the shape of a figure of eight. It was cordoned off with crash barriers and stacks of tyres. Cones and chicanes had been set out along one side of the track.

'Silverwood Motors are based near Birmingham, aren't they?' Scott asked Max, as they leaned on a barrier and watched a red Ferrari and a silver Lamborghini zoom onto the track. 'Why have they brought the Salamander all the way to Cornwall for testing?'

Max shaded his eyes against the sun. 'It's because they can test all the underwater functions here as well as the road performance. There's an artificial lake over there.' He pointed to a stretch of water beyond the track. A powerboat was speeding along in a plume of spray. 'And at the back of the compound,' Max continued, 'there's a private harbour where they can test the car in seawater ...'

Max's words were drowned out as the Ferrari and the Lamborghini roared past. *It's a good thing we left Drift at home*, Jack thought. That noise would have blown a fuse in his hypersensitive ears! Jack, on the other hand, loved it – the sound throbbed through muscle and bone to his very core. And the smell! He breathed in petrol fumes, burning rubber and oil. *Heaven*!

Now a third car had appeared on the circuit. Unlike the other two, it hardly made a sound, even though it was travelling at phenomenal speed. The air shimmered around it in a heat haze.

As the car whispered to a stop in front of them Jack let out a long sigh of awe. It sat low and wide and sleek, its black paintwork glistening in the sunshine, as slick as if it were wet. Air vents along the flanks gave it the menace of a shark. Jack grinned at Scott and nodded. The Black Salamander had *everything*: the raw power of a Bugatti Veyron, the style of an Aston Martin and the silent speed of a stealth bomber.

The doors opened upwards like the outstretched wings of a giant bat. For a moment Jack expected Batman himself to spring out, cape aflutter. Instead a tall man in white overalls eased out of the cockpit. He pulled off his helmet and raked a hand through his sun-streaked hair.

'This is Connor Jamison,' Max said. 'The Black Salamander's official driver.'

Jack had to stop himself bowing down in worship. Connor Jamison was only the sharpest new British Formula One driver since Lewis Hamilton!

Max clapped the driver on the shoulder. 'Connor is going to be the stunt double for the lead actor in Ocean Force. And I've got some immense stunts lined up for him!'

Connor Jamison grinned. 'I get to do all the dangerous stuff! Cool, eh?'

Just then a mechanic hurried over from one of the workshops to tell Connor that the new oil filters he'd asked about were ready. Scott and Jack listened happily as Connor discussed intercoolers and twin turbos.

Emily tuned out. She wasn't interested in engines. She just wanted to find out about the gadgets and the going-underwater part. As she gazed around she spotted Alesha Rahal hurrying towards them. A man in black jeans and t-shirt loped along at her side. His designer stubble and sunglasses gave him a cool-without-even-trying look, and a bulky camera bobbed on his chest with each step. Emily guessed he must be a reporter. Alesha was holding her phone to her ear. And what was that in her other hand? Not … a *hairbrush*!

Emily dived behind the Black Salamander. No one was coming near her hair with a brush! Even her mum had given up years ago! She peeked out and saw Alesha introducing the reporter to Scott and Jack. 'This is Shane Hazard, from *Motor Mania* magazine. We thought *Ace driver shows off supercar to local kids* would make a nice little feature.' She waved the hairbrush in Scott's direction. 'Now, where's your friend? A pretty face will widen the market appeal.'

Emily had almost crawled underneath the Salamander now. She could feel the heat radiating from the black metal. A little red light winked under the exhaust pipe.

Suddenly she heard a voice behind her. She looked round, preparing to dodge the hairbrush, but the voice belonged to a young man in a leather jacket who was sitting on a stack of tyres.

'Yeah,' he muttered into his phone. 'Connor Jamison is swanning around playing the big hero again ...'

The man paused and looked to the side. Emily realized with a start that his ginger hair hadn't been deliberately shaved into a punk style, as she'd thought at first, but was growing in patchy tufts. His forehead and scalp were horribly scarred down one side, the skin waxy and warped like a melted candle. 'Just because Jamison's got the film-star looks,' he continued, 'Silverwood fob me off with "back-up driver" and *he* gets Monaco and Hollywood!' He listened for a moment. Then he laughed softly. 'I know! Tonight's the night. Don't worry, I'll be there ...'

Meanwhile, on the other side of the Black Salamander, Connor Jamison looked at his watch. 'We need to crack on with the underwater testing in a minute.' He turned to Shane Hazard. 'Do you want to get a couple of quick shots of the boys sitting in the car first?'

Shane Hazard gave a thumbs-up. 'Sounds good.'

Jack couldn't believe his luck! He was going to get his photograph in *Motor Mania* magazine with the coolest car on the planet! His friends back in London were going to be so jealous! Surely any minute now his alarm clock would go off and he'd wake up to find this was all a dream. He reached out towards the Salamander just to check it was real.

Wee-wah! Wee-wah! Wee-wah!

Jack shot back and clapped his hands over his ears. The noise blared louder than a *million* alarm clocks! Security alarms were going off all over the compound.

THE ADVENTURE CONTINUES

Secret agent tests

•

Character profiles

•

Hidden codes

•

Exclusive blogs

•

Cool downloads

DO YOU HAVE WHAT IT TAKES?

**Find out at
www.adventureislandbooks.com**